HOUSE OF SEVEN MURDERS

TRANSLATED BY ALEX VALENTE

Cover design by Leaven Agency.
Book designed and typeset by Leaven Agency.
Edited by Keith Henderson.

Legal Deposit, Bibliothèque et Archives nationales du Québec
and Library and Archives Canada, 2nd trimester, 2025.

Library and Archives Canada Cataloguing in Publication
Title: The house of seven murders / Matteo Dello Schiavo ; [translated by] Alex Valente.
Other titles: Casa dei sette omicidi. English
Names: Dello Schiavo, Matteo, author. | Valente, Alex, translator
Description: First Canadian edition. | Translation of: La casa dei sette omicidi.
Identifiers: Canadiana 20250109646 | ISBN 9781927599631 (softcover)
Subjects: LCGFT: Novels.
Classification: LCC PQ4904.E55 C3713 2025 | DDC 853/.92—dc23

This book has been translated thanks to a contribution awarded by the Italian Ministry of Foreign Affairs and International Cooperation and the assistance of the Instituto Italiano di cultura in Toronto.

Printed and bound in Canada.
Interior pages printed on Enviro Book, an environmentally responsible paper containing 100% post-consumer recycled fibre, processed chlorine-free and manufactured using biogas energy.

Distributed by LitDistCo.

DC Books
5 Fenwick Ave., Montreal West
Quebec H4X 1P3
www.dcbooks.ca

MATTEO DELLO SCHIAVO

HOUSE OF SEVEN MURDERS

TRANSLATED BY ALEX VALENTE

FOREWORD

I have been on the *Statale 18* road that connects Naples to my father's hometown in Calabria at least twice a week up to the age of sixteen, when my family finally moved to Paestum to stay.

My father was unable to spend more than one week away from that place, and so we had a forced ritual of spending every weekend in town.

A few kilometres before the end of the *Statale*, its parallel road laps against the farmstead of Filette, in the municipality of Capaccio; beyond the fields, which are impenetrable until after the harvest, one can catch glimpses of the house of seven murders.

I have heard the story a hundred times from my father, then from other family members, all descendants of the main character, all telling the tale from his point of view as an innocent man.

Fate wanted that I would marry one of the victim's descendants, too, so that I may hear the other side from her family, the side of horror, the side of curses.

That's where the idea for this novel was born, trying to reconstruct the events, keeping the official documentation in mind (what was available to me, in any case) and everything that our oral histories could add.

The result is this novel, which starts from an event that actually took place, and well known to everyone in town, and becomes a story featuring yes real people and characters, but flights of fancy in dialogues, personalities, emotions, and thoughts.

Though a hundred years have passed since those events, I have changed the names of the people involved, so that current living descendants may not feel attacked or misrepresented. The historical characters, on the other hand, are unvaried.

I dedicate this book to my father, and to the love he harboured for his land: I don't remember him being a strong reader, but I like to believe he would have enjoyed this tale at least.

Pianosa Correctional Facility

Dearest Cousin,

I write to you with my deepest condolences for the tragedy that has befallen you. Oh woe! How are you capable of withstanding such unluck? And how about Aureste, wilting in a dark cell with no hope of ever gazing upon the Sun again? Surely though he is your brother you might (perhaps) ask yourself whether he truly is guilty or innocent and by such thought your conscience will remain untainted; who more than the author can truly ascertain guilt? Well, in this case, myself: I declare today such as I declared two years prior to the Royal Carabinieri *of that location, and to the King's Prosecutor of such institute. (This letter, and the statements therein, you may present as written evidence.)*

I state: Aureste is innocent of such deeds as he is accused of committing, and woe has cruelly befallen your house, akin to a lamb grazing in a verdant field when a pack of wolves descend upon it to feast. Poor folks! Henceforth I shall endeavour to the extent of my capabilities in the effort to clear the name of poor Aureste. I shall do all that is in my power to do so.

In the meanwhile, pray to our Lord Jesus, who will send the consoling angel when the time is come and will dispel the darkness and replace it with the shining rays of the Sun. As you can see, I have come to this prison of my own will to atone for my behaviour, and I send you my deepest.

Your affectionate cousin, Di Miele Giuseppe.
Pianosa Sanatorium (Convalescent House).
27 June 1931

The Cardon farmhouse lorded over the island of Pianosa.

The building had been outfitted as a sanatorium for the Correctional House in 1884 and housed all inmates who contracted tuberculosis from prisons across Italy.

It was a well-equipped hospital for pulmonary illnesses, and a place that all inmates – including those with lungs of steel – yearned for: rooms, food, and general quality of life were very different from those in the general population.

At the end of the hospitalization period, which everyone always hoped would last longer, patients were moved to the Convalescent House, placed in the Marquis Cardon Farmhouse, to see their recovery through.

Giuseppe di Miele, recently declared healed from that accursed cough that had threatened to rip his chest apart a few months prior, leaned out of the window of his cell. The window had no bars, but still drew a hard limit he could not cross. The sea below crashed and foamed against the sharp rocks; even with summer closing in, the water looked icy and hostile from up there.

What bothered Giuseppe the most was the sun rising from the water after he'd seen it set within all through his childhood. He thought back to his sea, the same one technically, but still the one he used to watch from a distance, from the Belvedere square in Trentinara. It was a light blue, that hue between cyan and sky blue, always calm and soft spoken, always just at the tip of his fingers. That's how he remembered it. He felt he had travelled through time – such a long time to flash through so quickly – to when he still knew nothing about life, and even less about death.

He picked up the letter again, thinking of how ten years prior he never would have known how to write his own name. And now the words had spilled forth from his soul. His restless, rotting soul.

Next to his cot, stained with the sweat-filled June nights, was an iron tripod, painted in the same yellow paint found in all hospitals, which must have been white at some point in its life. It held a small basin, also in lacquered metal, filled with clean water.

He stared at the water and dipped his hands into it.

A red cloud immediately spread through it, tainting its crystal clarity. Giuseppe could even smell the innocent blood he himself had caused to spill the night of 24th January 1922.

CHAPTER 1 - TEN YEARS EARLIER.

Tempone square in Capaccio owed its name to the place on which it was built, as the local dialect referred to the hillocks in the area as 'tempe'. The square itself was cooling in the scent-filled September breeze, the sycamores and holm oaks rustling intermittently, casting fractal shadows on the uneven cobblestones.

There would be small huddles of men, three or four each, gathering every Sunday standing and talking, flailing and gesturing in the emphatic southern way.

Giuseppe Di Miele and Giuseppe 'Calabrese' were sitting on a wall, to one side, chatting quietly, and keeping an eye on the centre of the square. Two young men, nineteen years old, both skinny and worn out, with nothing more than the clothes on their backs.

Di Miele was from Trentinara, a small town close to Capaccio, and had been working as a shop boy at the De Nicola farm for a few months. The other, Calabrese, had just arrived in town, and no one was entirely sure as to where in the Cosenza area he hailed from. He always looked worse for wear; he found it hard to hold people's gaze, and yet there was something in his eyes, images of something horrible that he had witnessed, or even caused.

The two had only just met, but were already close friends, helped by being the same age, of the same extraction, and with the same lack of means. Nothing to envy if there is nothing there.

"There he is," said Di Miele, with a slight nod towards Rosario de Nicola.

The two stood up from their spot on the wall and headed towards the centre of the square.

Rosario was a handsome man, in his thirties, tall for the time, with a fashionable moustache. He was wearing, like every Sunday, his good clothes, complete with a fustian vest and wide brimmed hat.

Business was going well that year, and all income made through hard work tasted better. Everyone worked hard at the farm, among the malaria-infested miasmas, the loneliness in the fields, and the few oxen with the plow.

And on Sunday, everyone would head into town.

After dropping off his wife Pasqualina for mass, Rosario would spend time talking to the other men; they'd talk about animals, harvests, business, testing the waters for new deals, and trade.

"Good morning, mister Rosario," Di Miele called out. "I hope you are enjoying your Sunday."

"Likewise to you, Giuseppe."

"I was hoping to introduce you to this friend of mine. His name is also Giuseppe, and he's from Calabria."

Calabrese was standing straight, facing Rosario, his head low as always, his hands torturing his cap.

Rosario offered him his hand, finding a tight, strong grip in response. An immediate positive impression, which caused a genuine smile to spread across his face, provoked by epidermal sympathy.

"You need a job, Calabrese?"

"That is precisely what we're looking to talk to you about, Rosario sir," Di Miele cut in. "If at all possible, Giuseppe would love the opportunity to work for you. Even just in exchange for room and board."

"Of course. Meet me tomorrow at five, at the Filette farmhouse. You can spend the night with Giuseppe if you need. Room, board, and a fair salary."

The two boys nodded – in respect and gratitude – and smiled as they started to move away. They were almost immediately called back by Rosario, who was holding out at five lire note.

"*Guagliu,* have a glass of wine on me. I'll be seeing you tomorrow morning."

Di Miele leapt for the money, and the tight smile on his face grew wider.

Rosario realized, in that moment, that Giuseppe the Calabrese had not said one word; he had just accepted a man into his house without knowing anything about him, not even the sound of his voice.

The two headed for Piazza Orologio, taking via Vittorio Emanuele, where Oreste Solimeno had his workshop. He was technically a cobbler, but also sold various foodstuffs and common items. When they reached him, Oreste was sitting on a woven chair, his chin resting on the back. Grin on his face, he studied everyone who walked past.

Oreste was a peculiar man. Some considered him a good man who tried to appear as evil as he could; some thought of him as a terrible man who tried his best to look good. Either way, a lot of people in town disliked him due to his arrogance, his *guappo* manners, and his overconfidence attributed to his having five brothers: the Solimeno.

They were respected and feared, secretly despised but openly revered, as nothing could be actually said against them, other than most of what happened in town involved them somehow. Among themselves, they never displayed much affection. In fact, their relationship was often tenuous, ready to snap at any moment when it came to business; blood always won out, in the end.

A bond stronger than any fight, than any unpaid debt, than any score unsettled. And so, it had been just that morning: Oreste, the cobbler-shopkeeper, and Enrico, his older farmer brother, had embraced in the middle of the road, one forgetting the alleged debt, the other forgetting the insult.

It had been, as usual, a nothing, a minor misunderstanding, which would undoubtedly be solved with a glass of wine or several.

Enrico shopped at his brother's store on the regular, paying once or twice a month, whenever it was more convenient to him. The receipt was written out on yellowed bread paper, held together by string. As not many folks were capable of reading or writing, these delayed payments allowed those with fewer means to acquire their food and goods, while also providing an easy opportunity for the merchant to inflate some of the prices. As a result, and to prevent that sort of behaviour, Enrico had demanded that his brother indicate the *age* of the purchases too.

"Age? What would that represent?" Oreste had objected, resentful that his brother would question his trade and honesty.

"You need to note down when I purchased the items too, not just the price."

Oreste had taken his brother's request as a personal insult, and they had almost come to blows. He had ripped out his brother's note and posted it on the front door, as a public reminder of Enrico's unpaid debt.

That morning, eaten by remorse, he had met up with *dearest Enrico*; they had embraced and had immediately forgotten all insults, injuries, and debts unsolved.

Oreste was still wearing the same smile, the smile of brotherly love, when he greeted the two boys.

CHAPTER 2

Giuseppe the Calabrese raised his glass for the last sip of Rosario de Nicola's five liras. They had both paired the wine with some black bread, but it still felt like barely a pebble in the vast ocean of their hunger.

"Who was that outside the shop?" Calabrese asked, bringing the last morsel to his lips.

"That's my cousin, Oreste Solimeno. He was the manager of the Filette farm until not too long ago. He had to let it go, he says, because of malaria. Turns out the owners, the Ferrandino, just didn't want him around any longer. Some even say that Mistress Giacinta herself handed the whole thing to the De Nicola, and that Eduardo and Carmelo Ferrandino would never have renewed the Solimeno contract. Not even for double the De Nicola price."

"How did your cousin take it?"

"Not well. He first tried taking the matter to the judicial board; then he started talking about revenge with anyone who would listen. Against both the Ferrandino and De Nicola, that is. The malaria story is his final port of call, a way to convince town that it was his choice all along, due to health reasons."

Calabrese listened carefully to Di Miele's words and added the logs of information about Oreste Solimeno to the wood pile in his mind. Ready, should he need them, to fuel the fire of his own ambitions.

This had always been his approach: gather as much information as possible about others; reveal as little as possible about himself, including his name.

Calabrese's interest in Oreste, however, was reciprocal. The cobbler was currently thinking about the two young lads who'd walked past him just now. The new one, especially: something about an intelligent glint in his eyes. He made a note to look into him further, to find out more about him from people in town. The boy might turn out handy.

Deep in these thoughts, Oreste headed home – it was almost time for Sunday lunch – where his seven children and wife Diomira were waiting for him.

Oreste was a good father and a doting husband (by the standards of patriarchal 1921 southern Italy), especially when he wasn't heavily intoxicated.

The issue was that he liked his wine. He liked his women, his gambling, his tobacco too. That's what made a man after all: you'd measure his worth by his vices, little or not, as everyone elevated them to almost virtues. An old saying from the 1700s claimed, these were the qualities of men of *ciappa* and consequence: men who had done so well for themselves that they could afford buckled shoes (*ciappa* being the buckle) and whose words were taken into consideration as they brought about consequences in life, for better or worse.

The square was emptying as people headed home for Sunday lunch. Giuseppe Di Miele and Giuseppe Calabrese slowly headed towards the road leading to the Filette farmstead. What awaited them was a two-hour trek, thankfully downhill along sweet, rolling, and shaded declines, which followed the twists and turns that led from the peak to the valley below.

Capaccio was connected to the valley by two roads. The first, more straightforward and steeper, headed towards the old city of Paestum. The second was a more sinuous thread lining mount Calpazio to the north-east; upon it were the ruins of Capaccio Vecchia and the Madonna del Granato basilica and, at the foothill, the old spring of Capo di Fiume. The road here met another, among reeds and canes, marshes and wetlands; this new road headed towards the sea, stopping by the train station and the farms dotted across the Piana del Sele in one direction, and the Rocca dell'Aspide in the other.

This is where both Giuseppes, with nothing in their stomachs than the memory of their food back in town, first spotted the farmstead, the large main building rising imposingly before them.

Calabrese started again towards it, but Di Miele gestured with his head to the other, the one set up for animals and workers such as themselves.

They stepped in as silently as they had been for the past two hours of walking, and neither the animals nor Vincenzo Pallotta who was tending noticed their arrival.

Vincenzino was a ten-year old, small, thin, very uninterested in what would be expected of a boy his age. Labour had replaced any interest towards play, after the last three years working as stable boy for the De Nicola. They had hired him more out of charity than actual need; what could a seven-year old effectively contribute after all? It was his mother's prayers and begging of Rosario that convinced the latter to take him on and to grant the boy at least one hot meal per day. Once or twice a week, Vincenzo would head back home to Gromola, a couple of miles away, but would never stay long; maybe even more so than when he left, it was hard to scrape a decent meal together. In fact, he had started noticing that his mother and sisters would look at him with a touch of worry, as if wondering how to feed another mouth during his visits.

For this reason and more, he'd choose to spend his Sundays at the farmhouse, alone, taking care of his animals, chatting to them as the friends he never really had a chance to make.

The rustling of hay startled him. He swung around but without looking up, and saw the shoes of the two new arrivals, barely six feet away from where he was standing.

Calabrese said nothing and looked at him with indifference and disdain. Di Miele attempted a smile and explained: "Vincenzo, this is Giuseppe. Rosario has told him he will be staying with us from now on."

Vincenzo took one step closer and offered his hand, like he had seen do between the grown-ups. Calabrese barely looked at him, but Vincenzo understood perfectly: there was a new hierarchy in the stables, and his place was somewhere below the oxen and barely above the rabbits.

CHAPTER 3

Pasqualina Arcella, as she was busy with her chores, kept casting glances out the fogged-up window, into the yard. She saw the new lad walking by a number of times and thought him familiar.

"Who's that new farmhand? He looks like he's a full-timer, no?"

"He's been here two weeks at least! Have you just noticed him?" Caterina replied.

The two sisters-in-law – the only two women at the farmstead – spent most of their time with each other, almost entirely out of necessity. It was definitely not out of pleasure, as their dagger-filled glares suggested, while they struggled to become the sole matron of the family.

Pasqualina was older by a few years; she was Rosario's second wife, and they already had four children together. This was enough, in her opinion, to make her the effective ruler of all things domestic in the De Nicola home. Not that the role actually mattered. There was plenty of work to go around, plenty of toil, and all decisions – the how, the what, the how much – fell upon the men. The women's duties were to push out heirs, bring them up best they could, and take care of the hearth.

Caterina Dalfeo, on the other hand, was twenty-four years old and possessed the rural, simple beauty of the farmgirl. Caterina received many a look, and she loved the attention almost as much as she loved that her husband Antonio – the younger De Nicola brother – was jealous.

"You immediately noticed him, of course," Pasqualina replied. "You probably went out of your way for him to notice you back, I imagine."

"Pasqualina, please, he's barely of age. I thought he was one of those temporary farmhands we hired once in a while; they spend the night here then leave. But no, I asked Antonio just yesterday as I saw this lad working for a few days now, and he told me that Rosario hired him full time. I see your husband has kept you up to date as usual."

Pasqualina did not reply to the cutting final words, as she knew her sister-in-law was correct.

"So, does he have a name?"

"I believe it's Giuseppe. He's supposed to be from Calabria, but I heard nothing else."

Caterina was not the only person in the dark on many of the details of Calabrese's story, despite the fair few days he had spent at the farmstead already. Just as he had initially done in Capaccio, he had kept quiet about his past and personal details, to the point that the welcome everyone had given him had already started turning into general, and obvious, mistrust. Who knew what secrets he actually carried, how was he so stoic and impenetrable? To avoid any consequences, people had started avoiding his eyes at first, and the rest of him soon after.

Oreste Solimeno, on the other hand, had explicitly come looking for him whenever Calabrese had headed into town. He was convinced that his first impression of the lad was all but confirmed by his refusal to share any more than was necessary: that kid could turn out useful for him, and he would stop at nothing to have him be part of his plans.

The perfect opportunity finally arose once the wind changed to the cold gusts of November. He watched him step into the inn, his collar high to cover his face, and wearing a military cape that no one had yet figured out how he'd acquired.

He sat at a corner table, away from the other patrons, and avoided them entirely as usual. Before he could even call to the innkeeper, Oreste was in front of him, scraping a chair across the floor, and sitting at his same table.

"Thirty-thousand lira."

Giuseppe arched an eyebrow but stayed silent.

"Do you know how much that is?" Oreste insisted.

"A lot of money."

"Precisely. It's also the amount that Rosario De Nicola made with the tomato harvest last year. Not that he doesn't deserve it, mind you. Everyone worked hard; it's only fair. But what's also fair is that I was the one to create that farm. I prepared the soil; I got in touch with the folks at Cirio. Then *signora* Ferrandino had her *piccio* moment, and I had to drop everything, come back here, and go back to fixing boots and shoes for these few souls in Capaccio."

Giuseppe was listening without interrupting, encouraging him to continue. His focus was entirely on the thirty-thousand lira.

"Giuseppe, I need you to be my eyes in Filette. I need you to tell me what's going on down there, what they're growing, who's buying, who Rosario is meeting with. He's a good man; I have nothing against him, but he needs to be careful. First mistake he makes, I'm taking it all back."

"Can your cousin Giuseppe not help you? Why are you asking me?" Calabrese replied.

"Giuseppe di Miele is an imbecile. You're made of sterner stuff. In fact, let me tell you something: the De Nicola will soon realise which one is the better between you, couple more weeks at most. And you will have the place you deserve at the farmstead."

"What's in it for me, then?"

Oreste frowned, his features growing darker. "You're already being rewarded by this conversation. Ask around, see what people say about Oreste Solimeno. Have a good night."

He stood up, gestured at the innkeeper who had been holding back in respect, and handed him a ten lira note. "Get some drink to my friends, Raffaè."

Raffaele, the innkeeper, vanished the money into the folds of his apron and cried out: "White wine for all on Don Oreste!"

The crashing sound of approval and gratitude and the rush to the bar covered Oreste's swift exit from the inn, as he revelled in the self-esteem boost his conversation with Calabrese had brought him – Oreste loved playing the part of the *guappo*, despite his actual character and physical presence. Calabrese on the other hand was less impressed, used as he was to letting things wash over him and shaking them off, afraid of very few beyond his true self.

He stayed at his table, waiting for the crowd at the bar to clear and take part in the free drink. He was, despite everything, considering Oreste's parting words. He would look into the Solimeno and see if they actually carried as much influence in Capaccio as he had been told so far.

Maresciallo Mancini had also had motive to look into the Solimeno family, on official business as the captain of the Capaccio Royal *Carabinieri.* Mancini was in his fifties, but still held himself together well, showing almost twenty years fewer with his wide shoulders and lack of belly. He only showed a few stereotypical signs of the *Carabinieri* officer – his large coiffed moustache, specifically – but he was well liked by the people and the institutions due to his thirty years of service and his intelligence and care in his duties.

Part of the latter, recently, had not been Oreste himself, but rather his brother Enrico: older, smarter, but equally hot-headed. His latest exploit had seen him smack the Eboli Tribunal magistrate square in the face, after a sentence of missing fulfillment on a contractual dispute. The two had met again, by chance, in Battipaglia, and the judge's hint of a smile had set off Enrico, who had forgotten his place, position, and relationship to the other man.

The whole ordeal had cost him two months of prison, a special warning, and the attention of the Royal *Carabinieri.* Ironically, however, the fact that he had slapped a judge in the middle of the street, plain for all to see, had also bought him a bit of a name and a reputation as a *camorrista*. By association, so it did the rest of his family, despite no one's actual affiliation with any clan.

The Solimeno family had people talking and had had people talking for years now. They had the reputation of being troublemakers, openly defying the status quo and the traditional powers in the area, so inextricably linked to the more rural regions of the Kingdom.

Despite the unification of Italy being sixty years prior, local families – much like many in the south – still held onto their fealty to the Spanish House of Bourbon, while openly professing loyalty to the current royals. After all, complaints are the prerogative of the poor, as the poor easily forget the hunger of yesterday as the hunger of today elbows its way in. Misremembering the past meant that many looked upon the previous rulers with fondness, turning toil into privilege, anxieties into passions, dried breadcrusts into fragrant loaves.

The Solimeno, on the other hand, had always been close to the new rulers, seeking out new status and positions, shaking off the taxation of blood and census demanded of the less wealthy. In either case, however, the old adage still applies: everything changes so that nothing may change, and so the rich retain their wealth; the common folk remain common, and the hunger of poorer families only grows. The result had been that the Solimeno were in the unenviable position of being not entirely liked by both the ruling classes, who would never let some upstart farmers join their ranks, and the common folk, who saw them as proxies for the new masters, and therefore better off than themselves.

What Mancini was pondering over, at this point, was a note from *appuntato* Bertolucci:

On the eve of 20th November 1921, Solimeno Oreste was seen in Raffaele's inn, entertaining a conversation with one Giuseppe 'Calabrese', currently employed by the De Nicola farmstead.

No further details available on the latter.

Solimeno left the establishment a few minutes later, in a clear state of distress, viz angered.

Mancini made a note to further investigate this Giuseppe, at least to confirm his identity, though he had no reason to think him a threat, given the young age. What was bothering him was what a newcomer and a *camorrista* might have talked about – and that Oreste Solimeno had left red in the face shortly after.

I will send Bertolucci, as soon as available, he thought. *In fact, I may pay a visit to the De Nicola myself, tomorrow morning.*

His immediate change of plan was suggested, though he would never admit as much, by the realization that he could exchange a few words with the lovely Caterina.

The plans were drenched, literally, the following morning: it had rained all night, and the new day brought more cold wind, making the water-filled road to the De Nicola particularly unpleasant. Not that it was pleasant to begin with, but the vehicles assigned to the Capaccio Royal *Carabinieri* were two bicycles, heavy enough to break a sweat on any minor incline. Just checking in on the farmstead would take him at least the best part of the day, between riding on the way down and walking the bicycle on the way back.

Mancini decided that, Caterina notwithstanding, the operation could be delayed after all: Calabrese would come back into Capaccio eventually; he would talk to the young man then.

Giuseppe, however, never did make his way back to Capaccio. Very few people saw him after that night, and those who did would never tell anyone anything ever again.

CHAPTER 4

Oreste had been right in his intuition about which Giuseppe had more influence over the other: in a matter of days, Calabrese had all but submitted Di Miele to his will, to the point that the latter would not set foot anywhere without his companion's approval. He had been brainwashed, some might say; Calabrese had found deep rooted hatred that Di Miele never knew he had.

"Look at them stuffing themselves," Calabrese would say, gesturing to the De Nicola family gathered for lunch. "We toil from dawn to dusk for a pittance, and Rosario gets rich on our labour."

Giuseppe Di Miele would nod in agreement, though this had been the first time he had noticed the difference between the workers and the masters: that's just how things had always been, how they were supposed to be. He'd always thought of himself as lucky, too, as he'd always had a roof over his head and at least a full meal per day. If someone was much better off than him, well, that wasn't his problem, as there were also definitely many who were much, much worse off too.

Calabrese had changed all of that. Everything the masters did, every crumb of luxury he might have never noticed before, now it all felt like an insult to their work, to the sweat they offered to the land as they toiled.

Calabrese would egg him on, with sideways glances, smirks, and half-spoken allusions, to clothes, to accommodation, to work, to women. Any time Pasqualina or Caterina appeared in their field of vision, Calabrese would re-focus immediately: "Why aren't we allowed to have a woman?" and "I bet Antonio De Nicola is getting lucky tonight," or "Look at her and her arrogance, always looking down on us."

The two women actually cared very little about the young farmhands. They cared very little about any of the workers, be they temporary or full time. They may have done so due to an order from their respective husbands, in order to keep some distance between the other men in the property. Antonio was particularly jealous of his Caterina; some would say with reason, too. She was young; she was beautiful, and more than one man had fallen for her; a lingering smile or look was all it took for even the more respectable men in town to entertain the idea of something more.

Giuseppe Di Miele's mind soaked up all of Calabrese's bitter comments. He'd take them and inflate them to the extreme. The kindly farm managers would suddenly become exploiting monsters, their small meals gigantic banquets specifically to mock them, their wedding beds a sinful dive of lasciviousness.

"I spoke to your cousin." Calabrese interrupted his train of thought, as if continuing a conversation they were already having. "Do you know how much your masters have put aside?" *Your* was an interesting choice for emphasis, as they were both employed together.

Di Miele looked up. "How much?"

"Thirty-thousand lira. We need to take care of this, of them."

The last two words clung to Di Miele's mind like ivy, but he did not initially pay too much attention to them. He had been too shocked by the enormity of the amount and the extremely unlikely possibility that his work might have contributed to it. His opinions changed with the wind, or rather, with Calabrese's words.

"Filthy bastards. They're getting rich with our blood."

He had swung from complete indifference towards his employers and gratitude for his position, to hatred for their every action, condition, or state of being. Calabrese, on his part, strung him along on a leash, effectively telling when and how to bark.

Christmas 1921 had been, for Vincenzino Pallotta, exactly the same as the previous year. As the old, colourful adage goes, it was not too dissimilar to a chicken coop ladder: short and covered in shit. He had spent the entirety of one day with his mother, who had welcomed him with the warmth and affection that the holiday demanded. The second part of the adage was fulfilled in plenty by the farm's animals, who did not care for the humans' celebrations, and had made the same deposits as any other day – meaning that Vincenzino had to catch up on his duties on the 26th, when he returned back to work. At least he had the memory of his mother's recent affectionate gestures, which had been the brightest part of the short vacation.

His mood changed swiftly over the following days: he wasn't sure why, but he could tell that the atmosphere was different at the farmstead, more tense.

The two Giuseppe had a strange light in their eyes, and a cruel smile peeking through their faces. They barely spoke, and when they did, it was only against the masters.

That word, 'masters', along with the tone they used to say it was enough to reveal the hatred behind their conversations, a hatred that had not been there previously.

Rosario, Antonio, Pasqualina, Caterina had always been called by name, by relationship or at what he thought they were to them: friends, even with their different roles.

For some time now, however, he had heard the two older farm-hands talk about them as a separate entity, as 'them' opposed to 'us', as if two opposing armies.

He'd even seen Calabrese doing something strange to a piece of wire, one time. He had twisted it upon itself, shaping it into a noose to attach to his belt. Similar to a carpenter's tool, he had then attached a small hatchet to it so that he could always carry it on his person, almost concealed under his military cape.

It struck Vincenzino as strange, as the hatchet wasn't a commonly used tool. The axe used for woodcutting was much bigger, unable to be carried around hanging from your belt. Even stranger was the fact that Di Miele had also started walking around with a hatchet on his belt, which he'd try hiding whenever he'd come across Rosario or Antonio De Nicola.

Vincenzo really wanted to ask them what it was all about, but he was terrified of Calabrese ever since the first time he'd seen him. So, whenever he'd meet him he'd lower his gaze or try to look really busy with whatever he was doing; more often than not, if he'd spot him in the distance, he'd change his route in order to avoid him and his murderous eyes entirely.

One morning, he was busy spreading manure on the property's outskirts and really needed to empty his bladder. It had been so cold the past few days, and it wasn't helping. The closest tree was about forty feet away, on a small hillock. Out of a bizarre sense of shame despite his age and conditions, Vincenzo preferred not to go about his business in the middle of the field, and so headed for the tree. From the top of the hillock, he spotted two men talking by the horse fence, a few hundred feet away.

He recognized one of them immediately: Calabrese, his back towards him, his military cape covering almost his entire body. He could not place the other man, though he seemed familiar: unusual for the area except for actual nobility, he was wearing a wide brimmed black hat, which obscured his features entirely.

The burned house was a homestead on the outskirts of Capaccio, though technically still part of the oldest section of town. It was, allegedly, from the turn of the millennium, and still bore the name of Monticello. The flames had claimed it two decades prior and had made it into a pile of rubble, only useful for a brief respite from cold winter windstorms. It was regularly used by passing shepherds and travellers, who would sleep and do their business here.

The night of 19th January 1922, it was being used by Giuseppe the Calabrese, Giuseppe Di Miele, his brother Pietro, and Peppino Farrese, their cousin. They were huddled around a haphazard campfire made from damp twigs. The two newcomers had been invited by the other two and shared the same disrepute as the latter. Calabrese had organized the meeting to involve them in a certain business that would take place shortly. He had learned through his usual source that they spent all their time together and cared for each other so much that they had ended up in at least one knife altercation. Farrese still bore the scars of that particular fight. They were definitely quick of hand, but not as much of mind – precisely what Calabrese was after.

"Friends," he started, "I want to bring you into a secret I have recently learned, and into a shared hope. The hope, my hope, is that once you learn of this secret you may share the same idea as me. An idea of justice."

The newcomers looked at each other in confusion, then at Di Miele, their expressions utterly baffled. Di Miele shushed them with a gesture and invited Calabrese to continue. He turned to Pietro, and asked: "How much is in your pockets, Pietro?"

"Fucking nothing."

"How about you, Peppe?"

"And how many hours did you work today?"

"Dawn to dusk."

"What about yesterday? And the day before?"

"The same."

"Perfect. So, you can see, plainly, how much your masters are exploiting you. You break your bodies every day, shivering through winter and sweating your eyeballs out in summer, and what do you have to show for it? Nothing. Not even a few coins for a drink with your friends. All you have is a gift from your masters, who have even convinced you they care for you."

"Thanks for reminding us we're nothing more than shit, Calabre'," Pietro cut in. "What do you want us to do about it?"

Calabrese pretended not to have noticed the interruption and spoke again: "My idea of justice is that, if we are given the opportunity to take back what others have made off the back of our labour, then we have a duty to do so. I have learned, from a valid source, that our master Rosario De Nicola has put aside, in his home, over thirty-thousand lira. Think about that. Thirty-thousand lira. An amount none of us would be able to make if we worked for ten years straight.

Our opportunity is in two days from now. I have learned, and this time with my own ears, that Antonio De Nicola will leave the farmstead for errands in town. Only Rosario, the women, and the children will be home."

The whole part about justice, about finding a moral justification for a less than moral action was probably just overly zealous preparation leading to this, he realized. His audience was not quite at the level of culture or education that they needed to quieten their conscience before committing an illicit act. Their needs were about their gut and gut alone, and that sometimes involved a few extra coins. He switched to the details of the plan with no other reference to ethics or morals.

"Even with just two women and one man, Giuseppe and I alone cannot take them. We need you. Especially considering the four children, who will cry and scream as soon as anything happens. This is the plan so far: when the family will gather inside the house for supper, Giuseppe and I will knock at their door with urgency, as if there were a fire. We will restrain Rosario and the women, through threats of harming the children if needed – then, the two of you come in from around the doorway. We tie them up, gag them, and search all over for the money. We will need to actually look, as I don't think it likely it'll be stored in plain sight. The house is big, but we'll have all night."

"What about after? What happens then?" Pietro, the more talkative of the two newcomers, asked.

"After that we split the reward equally, and everyone heads on their own way. We will have to leave Capaccio, Trentinara, and probably the Salerno province entirely, you understand."

"Good riddance," Peppe said, speaking for the first time. "I can't wait to leave this shithole. All it's given me is cold and hunger. I'm in."

"Me too," Pietro added. "No one will notice if I'm gone, anyway."

"We're set, then. Come to the farmstead two days from now, and wait by the low wall, next to the chicken coops. We will come from the barn, make a racket as we reach the doors, and as soon as someone opens, we threaten them with an axe to the throat. The other goes for the children; you sneak in and start tying up Rosario and the women. Then we search."

The four men stood up and nodded to each other. Perhaps due to the last crumb of honour left in them, no one shook anyone else's hand.

CHAPTER 5

Oreste Solimeno stopped by the site just after dawn. The labourers building the new house he was setting up in town were used to seeing him around, though he wasn't always consistent. Sometimes he'd be there before them, to speed them along; sometimes he'd arrive as they were picking up the tools, to check on their progress. Sometimes he didn't show up for two or three days, busy on another errand, and his brother Alfonso would come instead. It was Alfonso who spotted him at dawn, just as he arrived at the construction site himself.

"Oreste, already here?"

"Hello, Alfonso. I am very busy today, so I cannot come by later. Make sure this lot actually works hard today. I want the house done by Spring, so I can move in. Is Mastro Gerardo not here yet?"

Mastro Gerardo Vittorini was the foreman and lead contractor and had not yet arrived at the construction site.

"He'll be here soon; don't worry. He's probably dropped by the warehouse to purchase some materials. Mastro Gerardo is a very precise man."

"Very well. I'll be on my way, in that case. I have to go to the store, and then I need to find someone headed to Salerno. I have a letter for Raffaele Petti, the lawyer, and I'd rather he received it personally."

He only heard Alfonso's reply once he was already on his way down the steps of via Arenara Sant'Antonio. He walked swiftly, with small steps, his mind buzzing with a thousand thoughts. Oreste was not doing well, recently; he had been overambitious with the workshop, the new house, and a few legal issues, and he had lost a fair amount of money.

At least, thank God, his wife's dowry had brought them land on the northern side of Mount Calpazio; specifically, a wooded area around via Sferracavallo. The problem with land, of course, was that you needed to work it, rent it, or sell it to make it profitable. And as much as he had tried, he had not succeeded at being a woodcutter, nor did he care to learn. He would never consider renting or selling, either. He was a Solimeno, and the Solimeno had only ever bought, increasing their belongings, capital, and profit thanks to the labour of others.

That said, Diomira's lands were still enough solid ground to look his creditors in the eyes, unashamed, even if they weren't profitable right now.

He reached the workshop five minutes later, greeted a couple of passers-by, and sat down at his workbench, surrounded by soles, shoe uppers, and his swarming thoughts.

Reality was definitely taking a different shape than what he had imagined, but he felt more misunderstood than disappointed. And he was certain it was all due to his political ideals, most of all. He was too advanced for this town: he loved technological innovation, the power that he could never actually aspire to, the influential friendship of the new aristocracy which, unfortunately, was closed off against all other social strata. The same status quo had to be maintained: the poor with the poor, the rich with the rich, and new money neither here nor there.

All this was why he felt he had to behave like a *guappo* despite neither his heart, nor body, being entirely into it. This was why he knew he had lost the Filette farmstead. That damn farmstead. He had fixed it; he had brought it up to speed, and barely two years later, they had let him go. Cursed by that damn malaria and clear disapproval from the owners. And worse, now the fruits of his labour were being reaped by Rosario De Nicola and his brother! Thirty-thousand lira with a single harvest! Everyone knew about that by now too.

That amount was enough to finish the house. Another year with another harvest, and you could build an entire new house. Rosario De Nicola could easily build himself a palace, if this kept up. It also looked like the new farm managers from the hills were immune to those damned valley mosquitoes too, who avoided them to prevent spreading anything they might be carrying in their outsider blood.

His thoughts leapt from the De Nicola strong constitution to the shapely body of Caterina Dalfeo, inevitably, and then to *maresciallo* Mancini; he had noted that even the *carabiniere* had not been able to prevent him from noticing the young and lovely Caterina.

In fact, he was starting to grow jealous of the *maresciallo* and bothered by the clear distaste the latter showed towards him. Never mind that Caterina was married, and happily so. More than once, Mancini had stood in his way, due perhaps to the rumours of Oreste and his family being *camorristi*, perhaps to his brother Enrico slapping that judge.

These buzzing thoughts fuelled the bad mood he had been harbouring since waking, and they now ruined the rest of his work. Oreste jerked up from the workbench, checked his pockets for the letter to the lawyer, and got ready to leave again.

He reached for the cap he was wearing on his way in, but then hesitated over another hat he'd wear once in a while: a black one, with a wide brim. He smoothed it out and placed it upon his head on his way out.

CHAPTER 6

The De Nicola farmstead at dusk saw farmhands, labourers, and managers busy storing their tools used during the day.

It had been impossibly cold all day, and it didn't look like it would get any warmer overnight. The three daily workers staggered their departures, as the two Giuseppes and Vincenzo tried warming up by a small fire they had started in the far side of the courtyard.

Rosario De Nicola stepped out onto the balcony and did something he had never done before: he called to them and invited them into the main house. "Boys, come inside and warm up by the fire, maybe grab something to eat."

The two Giuseppes looked at each other. Di Miele was starting to panic, as things were already shaping up much differently from how they had planned. Calabrese, on the other hand, smiled reassuringly: the invite was clearly a fateful sign, an exhortation to act swiftly, a confirmation from Destiny about his intentions. He set off towards the house, Di Miele and Vincenzino in tow; the latter was the only one of the three that had interpreted the invite for what it was: a good opportunity to warm their limbs and fill their bellies.

The main door opened onto a wide hall, a large rectangular table at its centre. The far wall housed a roaring fireplace, and a tripod held up an enormous, blackened cauldron.

Three children, between the ages of two and five, were playing with coloured wooden cubes on a faded rug, not far from the fire. A girl a few months old was asleep, swathed in several woollen blankets and rocked in her cot by her mother, Pasqualina.

Caterina, her apron highlighting her pregnancy, was stirring the cauldron, which wafted out the smell of bean soup with probably, two or three pig trotters.

The three farmhands sat down by the chimney and instinctively reached their palms out towards the heat of the fire.

"It's really cold out there, boys. Warm yourselves up; then we'll have some food together," Rosario said.

The conversation barely ever started: the women didn't talk; the children would cry out once in a while; the guests were strangely quiet, too. They ate in silence at the table, and Rosario thought that perhaps the sudden invite had made them nervous, and they might have been embarrassed about not having had time to clean up after a long day of work.

After the meal, Rosario headed for the main door again, clearly signalling the end of his hospitality. "Well," he said, "It's quite late, and we have another long day tomorrow. Have a good night, lads."

Vincenzino was the first out the door, followed by Di Miele and then Calabrese, a hand under his cape. Rosario was about to close the door behind him, when he found himself nose to nose with two blood-shot eyes staring at him. Calabrese's hand moved faster than thought: the hatchet rose with a twist, and slashed into Rosario's throat, cutting through his jugular.

The man fell in gurgling silence, without even the time to bring his hand to his throat; the slash had been too swift. His knees landing on the ground were muffled, and no one inside the room noticed what had happened.

Di Miele, however, did. "What the f---" he yelped.

"Go, kill her!" Calabrese snarled back, pushing him back inside, towards Pasqualina. The woman had yet to notice her husband on the floor, his head barely attached to his neck by a strip of flesh. Instead of moving back to safety, she leaned over, to get a better look at what was happening. Di Miele could see the blood gurgling out of Rosario's body; he could smell its scent, and something animalistic inside him switched – he went into a frenzy. He pounced over to Pasqualina and hacked her skull in half. Blood and grey matter spurted out onto his already soiled clothing, and Di Miele stepped over her body as if a sack of waste. He started lashing and hacking at anything he could see in his way.

His hatchet hit indiscriminately, landing into the furniture, the trinkets, the poor bodies of the children. Di Miele was entirely out of control, moving as if in a trance, barely aware of his actions. He struck the cot with the baby girl, which swung and fell onto the ground, offering cover to her tiny body. The woollen blankets softened her fall, and her muffled cries from beneath the cot were more of shock than pain.

Caterina's cries, on the other hand, were loud, much louder than the general yelling and the children, who were terrified and did not understand what was happening. Di Miele's hatchet didn't care: it cut through their flesh, and the swift death was immediate relief to the fear and confusion.

Caterina had been at the opposite side of the room when the slaughter began. She had seen her in-laws and the children felled under the hatchet, and had only had the time to cry out. She froze in fear, as something warm dribbled down her leg. Her bladder, already strained by the pregnancy, had not withstood the stress. She saw Calabrese heading towards her, wielding his hatchet with two hands, and her survival instinct kicked in. She unleashed a furious yell and sprinted for the stairs to the upper floor.

Behind the heavy door opening onto the balcony was the area where hay and wood were stocked: reaching it and shutting the door behind her would keep her safe for some time – not even an axe could get through that. Twenty steps, it was only twenty steps.

She should've bounded up them, four at a time, to have any hope of reaching it. But it was dark, she was pregnant, and everything felt against her. Calabrese was upon her before she even reached the halfway point: he grabbed her by the ankle and dragged her back down the steps.

Caterina's face kept slamming against the wood as she had instinctively moved her hands to protect her belly and the baby inside.

She turned to face Calabrese, in tears, voice rough from screaming. "Giuseppe please! I'm pregnant!"

The young man stared at her, almost shocked at hearing his name. He hesitated for a moment, a spark of conscience and a crumb of mercy trying to squeeze through the horror. Then he moved closer to her face, smiled, and sniffed her neck, drinking in the smell of her fear. He raised the hatchet and brought it back down – it slid across her temple, cutting into her neck, and smashed through the collarbone.

It had been five minutes, at most. Everything was suddenly quiet. Di Miele's heavy breathing was the only sound in the room, as he crouched down in front of the bodies of the children he'd killed, staring into the distance, not even registering the corpses.

Vincenzino had frozen at the door, unable to move, to scream, to even breathe. His masters and their children had been felled, one by one, by the two Giuseppes, with no rhyme or reason that he could understand. He took in the slaughter and trembled as he met the gaze of Calabrese, on the opposite side of the room, staring right at him.

Vincenzo shook himself. With incredible effort, he forced himself to turn towards the outside, where he knew he'd be safe. Staying in that house, staying on the farm would inevitably mean being hacked to pieces. His first step was as heavy as a large boulder, but it cracked the dam open: every step after it became faster, and faster, his legs flying off before he could think about where he was going, and he was in the courtyard. It had been raining, and he now slid in the mud on the ground, almost slamming into the mechanical baler at the centre of the yard. The wooden contraption had two enormous poles used to leverage the hay, about three feet off the ground. Had Vincenzo been just a little taller, he would've slammed his head right into them; instead, he slid under, ducking slightly, and was back on his feet on the other side, ready to run again.

His lungs were burning from the cold air flooding them with each breath, a stitch in his side sending sharp pain across his body, but he couldn't stop. His eyes were slowly getting used to the darkness, and he spotted Pietro Di Miele and Peppe Farrese on the other side of the low wall around the courtyard. On the other side, he thought he spotted the shape of a man wearing a wide-brimmed hat, but he would never fully be sure.

CHAPTER 7

The two men had been in position for an hour already, after they had watched the day labourers leave the farmstead on the main road. They had arrived in silence, walking with their heads low to avoid being recognized, and quickly settled behind the wall as instructed by Calabrese.

They were expecting to see Di Miele and Calabrese running towards the house, playing out the whole fake fire scenario they had planned, forcing Rosario De Nicola to leave his house. Instead, time had gone by; their toes were freezing, and no one had even walked up to the De Nicola door.

They had almost decided to leave the whole thing and head home, taking advantage of the darkness and of the fact that no one had seen them, when the door suddenly flung open and Vincenzo Pallotta stepped out. Then the shouting, the crying, the sound of glass and wood breaking, voices cursing, and Vincenzo fleeing as fast as he could.

"What the devil is going on in there?" Farrese asked, more to himself than Pietro.

"I have no idea," Di Miele replied, "but God strike me if I don't take a look. Calabrese must have sped up the plan and got some work done already. Let's move it, or he'll get all the good stuff, and we'll have frozen for nothing.

Despite their nature as scoundrels and thieves, they had no way to know the depths to which the other two men had plunged inside the house. Giuseppe and Pietro Di Miele might have lacked the expected brotherly love, but the latter definitely did not see the former under any Cain light.

They swiftly but quietly moved closer to the open door, passed by Vincenzo who barely saw them, and once on the stairs, saw the slaughter before their eyes.

"*Madonna santissima*! What did you do?!" Pietro Di Miele was barely able to blurt out, as Farrese froze on the spot, falling quiet and pale. He started to turn to flee, seeing the merit of Vincenzino's idea, but Calabrese was in front of him, both hands on the hatchet.

"Where do you think you're going, Giuseppe? One more, one less – at this point I have nothing to lose. One more step, just one, and I'll cleave your head in two, see how empty it actually is. So let's just sit down at the table, nice and easy, and you can have some soup. Then we can get to work, as we planned. We need to go through everything in the house, grab everything we can, and most of all, find that money."

"But the children... the women..."

"A life is a life, and a life sentence is a life sentence, no matter how many you ended. The dead can't speak, so no one will ever know it was us."

"But the boy! Vincenzo, I saw him run away. He knows!"

"Yes. He's gone now, and I can't waste time looking for him. Where do you think he can go at this hour anyway? At best he'll stop in one of the old farmhouses until the morning, and we'll be long gone by then. But we need to get to work, now, so we can leave. The four of us should make it an easier task."

Somewhat convinced, the four men started moving around the room covered in fresh corpses. They initially tried avoiding as much of the blood as possible, but slowly grew accustomed to the horror they had unleashed on that cold winter night, as they rummaged through everything.

Pietro Di Miele and Farrese had found a burlap sack and were filling it with anything edible they could find. They had emptied the larder of all the sausages and *capicolli,* all the cheese, all the bread. Just enough to get through the winter, not enough to justify the slaughter. They were already numb to it: part of it was the hunger they always carried with them, which made any morsel the most attractive of targets.

Giuseppe Di Miele and Calabrese, on the other hand, who had already eaten, were searching for anything else, and still not enough to explain the killing spree. Calabrese shouldered the hunting rifle he found in Rosario's bedroom: a tilting double-barrel Cosmi from 1895, with a carved stock; Rosario had looked after it as a prized collector piece. Calabrese wore it the way he had seen the *Carabinieri* do and marched around the house even more self-satisfied.

They ran through the entire place, looking everywhere, pocketing bracelets, more or less valuable items, a couple of jewels. They found no money.

They started frantically moving furniture around, even pulling up the floorboards, dusted every nook and cranny, but nothing: the thirty-thousand liras were nowhere. Both Calabrese and Di Miele started to think that it had never existed, that it had all been a product of rumour and gossip.

In his hectic movements through the main room, Calabrese kept walking past Caterina's body though he never looked down, as he was too busy searching for the whole reason they were here, until a twitch, an almost imperceptible spasm drew his attention, and he leaned over onto the woman's disfigured face. He listened, and finally heard something that could be her breathing. He couldn't be sure, but was Caterina not dead? He placed his hand on the shoulder he hadn't hacked, and shook her, violently, as if to wake her. Initially to no reaction, then she started moaning, emitting raspy breaths – he hadn't killed her. Not yet.

Calabrese didn't flinch. Nothing could distract him from this lucid folly now. The hatchet was not on his belt now, but he did have a new weapon, the Cosmi rifle. He slowly, methodically shifted it off his shoulder, grasped the barrel with both hands, and slammed the wooden stock into Caterina Dalfeo's skull.

"She refused to die. I saw to it."

CHAPTER 8

On 25th January 1922, at noon, the Lord looked back down upon Capaccio and the Paestum valley. A warm sun rose in the cold winter sky, jarring with the rain and cold of the previous days.

The Filette farmstead was buzzing with more people than ever: news of the slaughter had run on the wind and everyone, from the neighbouring farms and from town, had come to see for themselves, as the horror was too much to believe.

The Royal *Carabinieri,* led by *maresciallo* Mancini, had been here for an hour already, created a perimeter, and had their hands full with keeping family members and locals from trying to get closer to the scene.

Mancini had had a field office set up, with a couple of chairs and a rough table at the centre of the courtyard under a hastily assembled canvas tent. He wanted to question the first witnesses, on site but still not on the spot, and also to prepare for the arrival of the Royal Prosecutor and the Commander from Rocca d'Aspide. They had been notified via telegraph and would be in Filette by the afternoon.

Outside – currently wide-eyed in terror and anticipation, afraid of the consequences of being the first person to arrive on the scene of the crime – was Pietro Monaco, a labourer from a nearby farm.

Pietro was a large man, used to moving with the grace of a bull in a china shop. That morning, he had been able to stand on an area of barely a few feet of gravel. He shifted his weight from foot to foot, trying not to fall from the memory of what he had seen and the tiredness that had taken over him since.

Mancini, finally, called for him, and the voice shook him out of the torpor his mind had slipped into to avoid thinking too hard about the scene inside the house.

"Monaco, come inside! Monaco!"

The farmer dragged his feet a little and tortured his old, threadbare cap in his hands.

"Please, Monaco, sit. Tell me everything you saw this morning; don't leave anything out. And then tell me what you did after you saw what you saw."

Mancini's tone was more due to his mood than the need to intimidate this particular witness. He knew that Pietro Monaco was nothing more than someone who had wandered onto the scene of a massacre, and who, like everyone else, had been horrified. Even so, he only ever called him by his surname, avoided any moniker, and never even alluded to his first name, so as to avoid any semblance of complicity or proximity.

"*Marescia'* it was horrible. Blood, blood everywhere, the child. Rosario, he was crying. Pasqualina, her head. Her head was smashed."

"Monaco, I asked you to sit."

"Yes sir, sorry sir."

"Start again; calm down. From the start: why did you go see the De Nicola this morning?" Mancini realized it would be easier to ask direct questions of the poor farmer. He couldn't expect a coherent and complete statement from a man who currently barely remembered his own name.

"*Signora* Angelina sent me here; she sent me. She sent me this morning to see how Antonio and Rosario were doing."

Antonia – mother of the two De Nicola brothers – was known to everyone as Angelina; this was a well-established local tradition, of naming a child after this or that ancestor on paper, only to call them an entirely different name in life.

The woman lived in a building not too far from her sons and would send one of her labourers (such as Pietro) every morning to check in on them and on her daughter-in-law, to see if anyone needed help.

"Very well. And you arrived at what time? Seven o' clock?"

"No, it was later. It was day already. Maybe a quarter to eight, I think. I came down from the side of the hill; it's easier to come through that way, but there was no one working, and I thought that was strange. Usually, Rosario and Antonio are hard at work by then, and Vincenzo has let out the animals too."

"Then what happened?"

"I called out. *Rosario! Antonio*! But nothing, no reply. Then I heard the cows, so I called Vincenzo. But nothing from him either. I headed to the house and halfway up the steps, I saw these streaks of blood, like after the slaughtering of a pig."

"What did you do?"

"I kept going, and I saw Rosario, first. Then his wife. Head almost off her neck. I turned around to run away *marescia'*; that was too much. I started crying out for help, and I heard a baby crying from inside."

"Did you go in?"

"Yes. It was chaos in there. I thought I saw Caterina at the back and maybe the three children, still, on the ground on the other side. The crying was coming from under a cot, upside down on the ground. I opened it up and there was the baby girl, screaming. I picked her up with her blankets and everything, and I ran back down the stairs. I don't know about the other children, sir. I couldn't bring myself to go back."

"They're dead," Mancini cut in. "The girl, however – and thanks to you, I should add – is alive. She was crying out of hunger and because she needed changing, nothing else. Then what did you do?"

"I ran like the wind; I was yelling and flailing with one arm as I held her in the other. I got home and told people what I saw. I left the child with the women, and I ran to the station to let the chief know. He called you, I think. Then I came back here with two others and the people from home, but then you arrived."

Mancini nodded, let Monaco know that he was free to go but should be available for further questions if needed. Once alone, he inhaled deeply and plunged his head into his hands. He wasn't new to the horrors of the world, but this one was a lot, even for him.

They had called him barely three hours prior and hadn't understood how bad the situation was from the first hurried reports. Then he'd seen it for himself. The war, his years of service against crime, hunger, and the hurt that people brought about should have made him more or less immune to this sort of thing. And yet, nausea had caused his stomach to seize up. Waves of nausea, every thirty minutes, almost perfectly regular. The tears had been more merciful, immediately pouring down his cheeks at the sight of Caterina, covered in blood.

He found her on her back, her legs up to protect her belly. He hadn't been able to look at her face and had looked away immediately – her beautiful face, now a formless pile of blood and flesh.

After the initial shock, his professional training kicked in again, and he immediately ordered a perimeter, started looking at the footprints, trying to understand how many had stepped onto that blood-soaked floor.

He couldn't tell. It was too much. The almost dry blood had print after print, the trails of where the bodies had been moved covered any others, and those who had been here since had just added to the chaos.

How many people had been present for the crime? How many people took part in the massacre? He needed to start with listing all the people who should've been alive and present this morning but weren't, be it because they were lying dead on the ground or missing entirely.

The two main labourers and young Vincenzo were the latter. Antonio De Nicola, freshly widower, was out there with the others, lamenting how it should have been him and not Caterina. He would speak to him later; he was more concerned to hear what Vincenzino had to say. They had found him at his mother's house in Gromola, scared and exhausted from the night spent in fear that what he had seen might happen to him.

The two Giuseppes, on the other hand, had vanished. Unless they were about to find them in a nearby ditch – unlikely – they were most definitely his first suspects. Had they done everything alone? Probably, Mancini surmised, as only one of the men was home and he had probably been surprised.

Mancini could not explain the ferocity, the bestiality of the crime. Two twenty-year olds, capable of all this? He knew all he needed to know about Di Miele: not a saint, sure, and had been born hungry, grown up hungry, and that had led him to a couple petty crimes. Never violence, never murder. What about Calabrese – in fact, who was Calabrese? He knew nothing about him, and this vexed him greatly. He had dismissed his own initial concerns, labelled him as unimportant, and he had probably made a big mistake that was now clashing with his years of experience.

The fact that no one else knew anything about Calabrese was not a great sign, either; clearly the young man was hiding many a secret. The Magistrate and his superior officers would reprimand him for his lapse in judgment and resulting negligence.

They would be right to do so, too.

CHAPTER 9

Maresciallo Mancini pressed his palms against his face again, took a deep breath, and prepared himself to keep questioning other witnesses.

He had been informed that Vincenzo Pallotta had been brought to the farmstead and was waiting in the courtyard. Two *carabinieri* were protecting him from the crowd who, more than being worried about a ten-year old witness to a slaughter, were pressing to find out more about the events firsthand.

Mancini gestured to his men outside the tent, and Vincenzo was brought in.

"How are you doing, Vincenzo? Have you eaten yet?" Mancini found his kindness again. The boy was shaking, and he didn't want to scare him more than he already was.

"Yes, your excellency." Vincenzo had taught himself to refer to his elders with all the possible epithets and positions, even if they didn't apply to the situation or people at hand. He had been taught, since very young, that he was a lesser; he was born below these other people, and when speaking to landlords, authorities, and masters, you should only speak when spoken to and delve deep into honorifics, such as "*Good morrow, your lordship*" or "*Fair eve, your excellency.*"

"Vince', do you think you can tell me what happened last night?"

"It was all so fast. We spent a nice evening together with the masters, inside his home. He had invited us in to keep warm for the night, have some good food; I watched the children playing with their wooden toys.... I wanted to join them too. But I'm grown up now; it felt strange."

"You're a young man, Vincenzo. You're right." Mancini did not want to rush the boy, who had started a long way away from the point: if he felt more comfortable, Vincenzo would reveal more important details he might otherwise miss.

"After we finished dinner, it was dark; master Rosario said goodnight. Giuseppe and Peppe stood up to leave; I was already at the door. As Rosario was closing the door – he had followed us to see us out – Calabrese took out a hatchet and struck Rosario. Then there was shouting and crying and blood, and Beppe leapt inside to strike the lady."

"Vincenzo, wait. Are you saying Beppe had a hatchet too?"

"They both had one, yes. I saw them for a few days, carrying around a hatchet on their belt."

"Please, continue."

"Calabrese yelled at Beppe not to kill them all. I've never seen Beppe like that; he didn't look like himself. He went in and he struck lady Pasqualina in the head; then he started flailing around. He hit the children too."

"Where was the other woman, Caterina?"

"On the other side of the room, far from the entrance. She cried out and tried running away, but Calabrese caught up and hit her too."

It took him five minutes. Mancini already had his two suspects, and they confirmed his suspicions too. The two labourers had become vessels of Satan himself – for no reason he could fathom – and acted out a slaughter like he'd never seen before.

"What did you do after that, Vincenzo?"

The boy had stopped trembling, but the question plunged him back into the memories of the previous night, and he started again, worse than before.

"I ran away. I was at the door already. I turned around and ran into the darkness. I don't know if they chased me; I never looked behind me. I stayed with Michele Pignataro, the farmer, until dawn, and then I went home to my mother."

"Vincenzo, you did great. You were great. I need you to listen carefully to me now; this is important: when Giuseppe Calabrese and Beppe Di Miele killed the De Nicola, was anyone else there with them? Did you see anyone else when you ran away?"

"No, no one else. Only the two of them. Just them."

CHAPTER 10

The road leading to the Capaccio cemetery wound upwards from the town outskirts, right after a small decline and a light bend to the east. It was sheer and difficult, embracing a side of Mount Soprano.

The De Nicola funeral, which had been attended by almost the entire town, had filled said road with voices whose volume increased proportionally to the distance from the coffins: the more quietly the closest family members wept at the front, the louder were the heated discussions at the back.

Among the latter, almost at the very end and almost hidden, were the Solimeno siblings. Vincenzo, Agostino, Enrico, Alfonso, and Oreste talked among themselves with smiles that jarred with the solemnity of the procession.

Mancini, further ahead with the family members, would keep turning around to look at them, trying to understand what they were talking about, to no avail. He didn't want his innate disgust for Enrico and Oreste, but he also didn't want to make a mistake as he did with Calabrese. Three days after the killings, the rumours had spread specifically in one direction: the slaughter was not the sole doing of the two new hires; someone else benefited from Rosario De Nicola and his family disappearing from the face of the Earth. Was this person present at the time? Did they order the killing from a distance? Were they still around, or were they even from the region?

Vincenzo Pallotta, unfortunately, was not helping the situation, as he had changed his version a number of times already.

He was probably encouraged by people demanding to hear a story they had already made up for themselves, and he had brought two other people into the story on a second and third questioning: one Antonio, and Corrado Giovine, from Ponte Barizzo.

The two men had iron-clad alibis and after two hellish days, had been able to prove they had nothing to do with anything that had happened. Vincenzo, clearly, was floundering and only needed a minor nudge to change his story one more time.

Mancini was pondering all this as he reached the burial site in the Capaccio cemetery, his head swimming with the unease of the events of the previous few days.

The family had chosen a slightly elevated spot, compared to the other graves. The coffins were lowered in a single grave, those of the adults first, and the small white coffins to follow.

Mayor Lombardi talked for a good fifteen minutes: a speech mentioning how never in history had something this awful taken place, that he had full trust in the Prosecution and the Royal *Carabinieri,* that those responsible would be punished, and that if a Capaccio resident were among them, the entire town should shun them. Such an act would bring shame upon their family, upon their community, one that could never be washed away.

Lombardi was genuinely incensed, though his experienced politicking inevitably led his funeral speech into a small election speech.

"Capaccio Town Hall will take on all financial burdens. We will be close to Antonio De Nicola for all his needs, and I promise you that my administration will aid and assist the investigation efforts to bring those responsible to justice."

Unlike usual political promises, the pomp and circumstance of speechifying gave way, within a few days, to the tangible reality of facts: on February 4th, he had commissioned the commemorative monument, a reminder of the awful crime:

HERE IN MARBLE
AS IN OUR HEARTS
ARE THE MEMORIES OF
DE NICOLA ROSARIO
WIFE AND CHILDREN
SISTER-IN-LAW DALFEO CATERINA
BARBARICALLY TAKEN UNTO DEATH
BY KILLER AND SAVAGE HAND
THE NIGHT OF JANUARY 24, 1922
THE TOWN REMEMBERS
IV FEBRUARY 1922
UNDER MAYOR A. LOMBARDI

As the days passed, the interest – both among the people and the institutions – did not wane. The events were brought up at any moment, in any context; new details were added with no regard for the truth; new theories were cooked up. The commonly agreed upon detail was that a third hand had directed the two Giuseppes, even a fourth; many, more or less directly, were pointing at Oreste Solimeno.

Oreste was either unaware or intentionally ignored these veiled accusations, as he considered himself above both the law and public allegations. From how he saw things, suspicions were more based on personal feuds and distrust after all, and as a braggart a few years from now would say, *many enemies mean much honour*.

As more time went by, however, the rumours did not fade either, and several written allegations were sent to the authorities involved, all rigorously anonymous. The desk of the judge in charge of the investigation was piling up with all sorts of written accusations against the Solimeno siblings and Oreste in particular, to the point that the Prosecutor was forced repeatedly to question what he fully believed to be a useful scapegoat, and eventually to lock him up in a *Carabinieri* cell despite lack of any evidence.

The pursuit of justice did not cease: each new letter revealed a bitter yearning for vengeance that not even unlawful incarceration had fully quenched. Anonymous requests demanded to strike at others that still had not been involved and tried swaying the judge's actions under several promises and exhortations.

"*Your most esteemed Honour. You have started upon the right path. And yet you harbour a snake in your own home and cannot see it? When will you deal with Agostino? When will you remove the key from the cell lock? His brother knew everything his brother had done from the start, and hid in the shadows...*"

"*Please note that all three Solimeno brothers are insulting the witnesses you have heard, telling them that they have control of all of Capaccio, even of the Institutions, and threatening Magistrate and* Maresciallo *saying that should the latter ever show their faces, they will deal with them...*"

"*Your Honour. Our trust in you is great. Please deliver us from a clan of* camorristi. *Avenge the slaps that Enrico Solimeno dealt to your colleague. Read of his trial! All the brothers are compromised now because of their insults! Please help us and we will help you with new information as it happens.*"

There were many such letters, and more still, almost as if everyone in Capaccio had realized they loved to write. And yet, no real arguments or proof, and Oreste's incarceration was slowly loosened.

He was allowed to move freely around the rooms of the *Carabinieri* barracks; his family was let in to bring him meals, and he spent hours playing cards with those who were supposed to be his jailers.

His wife Diomira, after the initial shock of the arrest, had processed everything as another quirk of her husband's fame. Despite having only recently given birth to Tecla, she regularly, almost daily, walked up to visit him, followed by a short line of her children.

Oreste acted as host for each of these visits. He let his wife sit, stroked his children's hair, played with the younger ones, and chatted with the older ones, showing a serenity and calm that he never really had at home. He never touched upon serious topics and joked about them with his eldest, Filomena and Antonio. He reassured them that when – not "if" – he would be home again, they would throw a party for family and friends, the same friends who had currently disappeared, but would inevitably return as soon as the dust had settled.

Filomena, his eldest daughter of fifteen, hung on every word her father spoke: she was madly in love with him, and had been shaken more than the others by everything that had gone down.

Antonio, on the other hand, took his father's reassurances from the height of his thirteen years of age, with the same attitude he had towards his studies, light, unserious, but still very proud to currently hold the title of man of the house.

Eleven-year-old Caterina aside, the other children were too young to understand what was actually happening, except maybe for the fact that they saw more of their father now that he was in jail, so to speak, than when he was at home.

CHAPTER 11

Mancini unfastened the button on his braided collar, which had been cutting into his chin. Despite his many years as a *Carabiniere,* he had never gotten used to that particular form of torture. Not the cartridge bag, not the cartridge belt, not the bayonet – the worst part of his uniform was the collar. He was certain they had designed the points to keep them all awake. He didn't need them, of course; in fact, he needed something to get to sleep in the first place, as the investigation had deprived him of sleep entirely.

He had never liked Oreste Solimeno, but he could not keep him incarcerated for long without proof. He had listened to the rumours and the written allegations claiming Oreste's presence at the crime scene, his interest in regaining control of the farmstead, and the attention he had directed at Caterina Dalfeo. The truth of the matter, however, was that he was a cobbler, and he posed as a *camorrista,* but there was no proof against him on this crime.

The only thing against him was that he had no alibi, as no one remembered seeing him anywhere on the night of January 24th, which was not enough to pin a whole slaughter onto him, even as an accomplice.

It was clear by now that the actual killers were Calabrese and Di Miele. Vincenzino's statement was the main piece of evidence, even if his reliability waned with each new detail of what happened after the actual killings. All he needed to change his story was to ask him a question in a slightly different tone.

It was also clear that at least two more people had taken part in the looting and stealing that followed: too many items were taken and too many footprints were left. There was no clarity as to who those other two people might be, what their role was in the whole ordeal, if they were still around, or if they had fled like the two Giuseppes.

As for the De Nicola family, all statements and all comments gathered so far had painted a perfect group of people, almost saints, with no enemies and whom everyone liked. Antonio De Nicola had confirmed all this, even though his own reputation was getting a little cloudier, be it the strange coincidence of him being away precisely at the time of the killing, be it the matter of the thirty-thousand lira – were they stolen? Did they ever really exist?

Antonio claimed he knew nothing about the money, and he should've been the one to know as he was the one taking care of the family book-keeping. He was a widow, that was the only concrete fact at this stage, and he was visibly heart broken. Mancini was reluctant to consider him part of the perpetrators simply because he hadn't been killed along with his family.

It was currently past midnight, and Mancini was rotating these thoughts in his mind, still at his desk in the barracks, in the dim light of the oil lantern; Oreste Solimeno, prisoner, was blissfully asleep a few metres away.

The following day, when the sun was still high in the sky, though barely warm, Enrico Solimeno showed up at the barracks. His usual gait was that of someone who believes the world should make way, half a cigar between his lips, and a hat tilted upon his forehead. That day, instead, his features looked tired, with heavy bags under his eyes from lack of sleep; with an attitude that surprised the *Carabinieri* at the door, he asked to speak to his brother. He was left alone with Oreste – yet another concession against the rules of incarceration – and he drew up a rickety chair, sitting on it legs wide.

"Oreste, things aren't looking good," he said, without a greeting.

"Rumours are piling up; there are statements against you, confirming you spoke to Calabrese on more than one occasion; Di Miele is almost family, and you're the only one who could have any ill sentiment towards De Nicola."

Oreste stared at him and tilted his head. "I knew all of this already, Enrico. Do you have any news for me?"

"Anonymous letters, one after the other. They're dragging the whole family into this mess. If nothing changes soon, if something doesn't come up that changes the investigation and directs it upon someone else, they're going to arrest all of us. You, me, Alfonso, even Vincenzo. I heard they want to transfer you to Salerno, because there's too much being built up against you."

"Too much? Too much what? They have nothing! There's nothing they can have! People don't like us? We knew that. But there was a slaughter, Enrico. They want to pin a slaughter on me because the town needs a scapegoat. What am I supposed to do with that?" He sighed. "What about the lawyer, did he have anything to say?"

"I saw him two days ago. I can't just up and leave for Salerno every day. He told me to stay low and not worry, not even about the boy's statements; they're leading them nowhere. His face told another story though, and it did nothing to convince me."

Enrico's words, his worried tone, had changed Oreste's mood entirely. After a restful night of sleep, he had woken up with a spring of optimism about him. Now his day had darkened. What awaited him was a life set to the routine of prison in the Salerno Penitentiary, and he was more doubtful he could avoid it now.

Until a few minutes ago, his plan had been to wait and do nothing. The lack of evidence would mean the bubble would burst sooner or later, but now his brother's concerned expression was suggesting a number of different scenarios. He had to act quickly and not keep wasting time playing cards with the officers in the barracks.

He bid farewell to his brother, lay down across the low table in the cell, and started thinking.

Can a human brain be so clouded that they do something stupid, following no rhyme or reason? Of course. Can a thinking person make an instinctive decision, which makes no damn sense? Certainly. It happens every day; we see it all the time. Can this decision, then, condition and taint the rest of that person's life, for better or – more likely – for worse? Naturally. Any event leads to more, sometimes bigger events, even the smallest, just like a snowball starting at the top of a mountain turns into an avalanche, and it tramples over everything.

What this meant for Oreste, a few hours later, was that he made a choice that was decidedly unwise, decidedly foolish, definitely irresponsible. That same evening, taking finally advantage of the lax security around him, Oreste Solimeno put on his shoes, and without even tying them up or picking up his coat, escaped.

The door leading to the lobby was wide open. Same for the cell door. The prisoner had vanished. *Carabiniere* Giuseppe Fallacara da Bitonto stayed very still, cards still in one hand, glasses and bottle of wine in the other. For a moment he wasn't sure that Oreste had left. He thought he might still be in his cell and that his sight was being tricked by some unknown force.

He was also lying to himself; he knew it, and he knew he could see perfectly.

The cards scattered to the air; the glass shattered on the floor, and thoughts of Court Martial and military prison forcefully made their way into his mind.

He looked out the door and saw Oreste running down the hill, uneasy on his thin legs and on the rocks that jutted out between weeds and thistles.

"Solimeno, stop! By God, stop running!" he shouted, heart in his throat, halfway between pleading and threatening.

Oreste had barely made it a few metres and heard him very clearly behind him, but made no sign of stopping, nor did he have any intention to do so.

The sound of broken glass and Fallacara's cries had alerted the whole barracks, and both Mancini and Bertolucci had thrown themselves after the fugitive.

It took barely two minutes to catch up, as Bertolucci leapt like a deer and jabbed his musket into Oreste's back.

"You idiot! You just signed your own death sentence."

Mancini was panting heavily, his heart beating hard against his ribs.

"What on Earth were you thinking? How did you see this going, you stupid *guappo* wannabe?"

"Marescia'," Oreste replied, resignation in his voice. "I'm giving you the culprit you need, even if I did nothing. The truth is that you're so incompetent, and you'll never find out who did it. So, you're taking it out on me, to make the people and the papers happy."

"Solimeno, I swear to God, you need to shut up. I don't want to hear another word. Bertolucci, cuff him. Those don't come off in his cell, either. He has to call us if he needs to piss, and he will piss when we want him to, unless he wants to wet himself. Then get Fallacara and come see me, both of you."

Fallacara, who had stayed back, heard his name and froze on the spot. He knew he was in trouble and that there would be consequences. He had been lucky that Oreste had escaped just a few moments before Fallacara was on his way back from the kitchen, so they'd captured him again. But that had been sheer luck. Five minutes earlier, and Fallacara would have lost his position, and maybe even his freedom.

"Commander," he started. Mancini glared at him.

"Fallacara, ten minutes, my office, with Bertolucci. You can say what you have to say there, if I allow you to speak."

Mancini wanted to cover up that whole escape attempt. Even if they had taken care of it immediately, it still revealed their incompetence and negligence. Even if the error was entirely Fallacara's, he knew it could have been anyone else, as he had allowed Oreste Solimeno's incarceration to feel more like a guest stay than prison proper. Still, Fallacara shouldn't have been stupid to the point of leaving open the cell door to go to the kitchen, for a pack of cards and wine of all things. Then there was the most important part of it all: reporting the prisoner's escape and immediate recapture meant – once they'd removed the lack of professionalism from the equation – a sudden turn in the investigation: Oreste had basically confessed without saying anything.

It was inevitable, then, that the Royal Prosecutor be informed of what had transpired, that the documentation on Oreste Solimeno be updated to reflect them, and that the number one suspect in the De Nicola murder be transferred to a real prison, forty kilometres away, to experience some hard and proportionate measures.

Fallacara would have to take most of the blame, and in the best case, he would be transferred to the other side of the Kingdom of Italy, hundreds of kilometres away from his beloved Apulia. He always talked about wanting to move back there eventually.

When the two of them, both standing outside the door, were allowed to step into Mancini's office, the latter had already made his decision: he would hide nothing, report everything, even if it meant taking a blow himself. Not identifying Calabrese, then a massacre in his jurisdiction, and now the escape attempt of a suspect in his custody. He would have to face some hard questions, but the choice was made. He would call the lieutenant in Roccadaspide that same day, inform him of everything. It was the only way to find the culprits, see they met justice, including Oreste Solimeno, and bring some solace to the families and memories of the victims.

CHAPTER 12

When the animal transport that was used for prisoner transfers – and that everyone insisted on calling an armoured car – turned onto via San Francesco in the old Salerno city centre, the lulling buzz of the wheels turned into a series of jolts and bumps, due to the poor condition of the road. It woke up Oreste, who had fallen asleep during the long journey, thanks to the darkness of his area and the general heat. He would've liked to have stayed alert, mind at the ready, as things were taking a strange turn; not even his lawyer's reassurances, the lack of evidence, and the investigators' incompetence seemed to soothe his worries. He looked out through the narrow slits on the side of the truck and was met with the looming shape of the walls of the Penitentiary.

At regular intervals on the yellowed stone, at a ridiculous height from the road, small windows appeared, covered in sturdy and thick bars. The sun outside barely made it through the ancient streets, and Oreste thought that it definitely could not make it through the windows.

And that's when fear struck him.

The complex was laid out across three floors, each originally a monastery. The San Francesco monastery had been built in 1222 and had been home to the Frati Minori; the San Pietro a Maiella and San Giacomo monasteries had been founded in 1332 for the Celestines. After Napoleon's clamping down on monastic orders – he considered religion and its institutions as a distraction – they were both converted, in 1807, into a men's prison. Santa Maria della Consolazione became a women's prison.

They were, therefore, ancient buildings, their walls imposing and their cells tight and damp, with barely any sunlight on the best of days. Perhaps perfect for their originally intended guests and dwellers, but not as much for the present-day inmates, who – much unlike the original monks and nuns – were more likely to curse and blaspheme the name of God. His was the fault for their guilt, for their own actions, and the consequences of those actions, or so they seemed to believe.

In this unhealthy environment, in which tension and neglect were palpable as soon as one entered, Oreste Solimeno took his first unknowing step towards never seeing freedom again.

"Did you see him? Did you talk to him?" Mancini looked up from his cards and started asking questions of Bertolucci before even inviting him to sit. His concern was obvious.

Bertolucci removed his cap and took a seat without waiting for an invitation, hoping that his friendship with his superior officer would excuse his behaviour.

"I saw him, and I spoke to him. It wasn't easy; everyone was paying attention to us. It felt like Salerno is almost entirely inhabited by folks from Trentinara and Capaccio; every other face was someone we recognized."

They both knew who the other was referring to; neither needed to name him. Bertolucci had just returned from the Salerno Penitentiary after overseeing the transfer of Oreste Solimeno, but the subject of their conversation now was the individual whose statement had contributed directly to the former's incarceration. They were talking about a criminal, a frequent guest of several penitentiaries, who spent more of his time in prison than he did outside of one: Gaetano Cifuni, subject of multiple sentences for crimes of theft, extortion, perjury, and obstruction of justice.

The Royal *Carabinieri* had relied on him to garner more information about Capaccio, any gossip between the various inmates, and any connection between those inside and those who had yet to visit one of these establishments – despite fully deserving to.

He was their mole, their informant, the one who served justice (and himself) by keeping his ears to the ground, his eyes peeled, and when he had nothing to offer, he made up stories and details instead according to what people wanted to hear.

"We made it just in time," Bertolucci continued. "One more month and we would've missed him: Cifuni is about to be let off, and he might not make it back to Salerno."

"I have my doubts about that," Mancini replied. "The only reason for that sort of individual to stay out of prison is taking a bottle to the head or a knife to the ribs."

"That's what I mean. We may have to head up Capaccio directly next time, the cemetery specifically. In any case, I was able to tell him what I needed to. He has done a lot for us already: his information about Gaetano Farrese was crucial. He will need to befriend Solimeno next and let us know everything he finds out, best case scenario, a full confession."

Farrese and Cifuni had spent three or four months together in a cell, had become friends, and Farrese had told Cifuni about his part in the De Nicola killings.

Cifuni, leaning into his snitch nature, had forwarded that information with a couple extra flourishes and added details, to make a better show of it. Farrese had told him that his brother Giuseppe had taken part in the events, if not as a killer himself, at least as a "shameless jackal partaking of the looting that immediately followed the heinous act."

The result of this passing along of information, though never confirmed from the original source, was that from watching over the sea from Trentinara, Giuseppe Farrese found himself looking at the sun through bars of a cell in Salerno.

He had been questioned like never before and had even been shown the edge of the hanging block – a much better end than a life sentence. The threats of branding were paired with those of constant abuse within the prison for the next twenty years unless he said everything the investigators wanted him to say. And Giuseppe spilled everything. For the first time, an eye-witness raised the name of Oreste Solimeno as someone present on the night of January 24th 1922, on the scene of the slaughter; he was singled out as promoter and instigator, and in a retracted statement, even placed as one of the killers.

The contradictions however were too many, and Bertolucci had spotted them all. Farrese's statements had also not been enough to incriminate Oreste – the latter's escape attempt was what pinned down his guilt, which would otherwise have remained hear-say and accusation.

"I still don't get it, sir. There are too many details that don't make sense. Why would Gaetano Farrese tell his cellmate that his brother, his own blood, is part of such a crime? Is Gaetano Cifuni that reliable now? I wouldn't let him walk my dog, never mind trust him with something this big. And what does Cifuni do with the information? He sings; boy does he sing. And once we have Giuseppe Farrese in custody, he tells us that there are two, then three, then four accomplices to the crimes."

"What else do you need to *get*, Bertolucci? We have a statement from someone who was present at the time, who saw and took part. If you start to scrutinize every detail of every statement, of course there will be missing links and contradictions. These men can barely write their own name, string together two thoughts; I don't expect them to be consistent or coherent for that matter. The crucial part is that now we know Oreste Solimeno was present; we don't need to know if he did it; we know he instigated it, and that's enough. And it's clearer by the day that he had to be, as he's the only one who could profit from it. He tried escaping, too; don't forget that. If he is as innocent as he claims, why run away?"

Bertolucci did not reply, but did not seem convinced. He knew that his superior officer had it in for Oreste, and had it been up to him, he would have already hanged.

He stood up again, pretty certain he was an active participant in a massive judicial error. He saluted the *maresciallo* and left the room.

CHAPTER 13

Federico Mollo often thanked the heavens for having learned to write and count when he was younger. These qualities, not common at all around the prison, had allowed him to avoid the harsher types of labour, those made of hours with a spade or pickaxe on a good day, or with hands in a toilet on the bad ones.

He, on the other hand, had landed a desk job, a position that allowed him to stay cool in summer and warm in winter, where you found out things that most never knew, and made important friends who might even shorten your stay in that place.

There were only a few months left until his release, and he had been working for the past six in the Treasury, as secretary for the auxiliary ledger. His notes in the book were also for himself, especially if they meant anything special or could be made to do so: he didn't want to lose his post, and he would never tell who gave money to whom, and how much someone might have made that month.

There were often strange movements anyway, and with all the miserable conditions of several prisoners, it was not uncommon for someone's name never to even show up in his book.

That day, however, Federico could not but notice that on "the eighth day of the month of September of the year 1922, the inmate Gaetano Farrese receives Liras ten (10) on behalf of *Maresciallo* Mancini of the Royal *Carabinieri.*" Usually, external money was sent to inmates by lawyers, who acted as proxies for their families. This was strange: a *maresciallo,* someone who had nothing in common with an inmate other than maybe being the reason for the inmate to be here in the first place.

Stranger still was the fact that this was not the first such payment (and he remembered them all): Mancini had sent ten or fifteen liras regularly to both Gaetano Farrese and Gaetano Cifuni. Had Mancini lost his mind? Had he chosen to waste all his salary on charitable donations to the Salerno inmates? There were only two possibilities, according to Mollo: Mancini was acting as proxy for a family member, as they were all from the same place, who was concerned for their distant kin to the point of sending their entire savings, or the money was payment for some service that the two men had provided or would provide to Mancini.

This one time, Federico Mollo found himself unable to keep quiet. The next time he saw Gaetano Farrese, he openly told him what he'd discovered. He was originally planning on chatting, maybe some light ribbing, without prying or asking too many questions, but Gaetano's reaction was surprising and out of proportion, and it confirmed Federico's original tenet: keep numbers to himself, always.

When it happened, Federico was just outside wing 7, where Farrese was assigned. He saw him through the bars. "Farrese, congratulations! You found a state-paid job!"

"Mollo, what are you talking about?"

"Come on now, don't play coy. The money comes in regularly; it has to be a salary. Both you and Cifuni, too! The Kingdom of Italy has been hiring, huh?"

"What the fuck are you talking about? A salary? Cifuni? It's barely seven in the evening and you're already on the wine?"

"Sure, I'm the one drinking. So, did I make up the name Mancini too? Did I imagine that too?"

"Shut the fuck up! You're lucky that I'm on the other side of this fucking door, or I'd have ripped your tongue out by now!"

Gaetano Farrese was furious. If his intention had been not to let anyone else know about the money, the result was completely the opposite: everyone in the area had gathered around the door to hear more.

On the other side of the door was Raffaele Normanno, the shift guard, who hadn't realized the severity of the situation and approached the door to let the inmates out for their evening hour. The heavy gate was opened, only just, when Gaetano charged headfirst with the clear intention to strangle Federico Mollo.

Normanno, used to the altercations of the prison, noticed the murderous intent and stepped aside, swung his arm up and elbow into his throat, grabbing his other arm behind his back.

It was too late – everyone knew now: Farrese and Cifuni were paid by *Carabinieri,* which meant they were probably informants; Mollo couldn't be trusted with secrets, so he had to move out of his post.

Farrese and Mollo, the two people who most should've kept quiet, were the two people responsible for the scene, and for the loss of credibility and privileges within the prison itself. Oreste Solimeno, on the other hand, barely noticed what had happened, as he had decided a while back that he would remove himself from all communal moments and other inmates' business. Little did he know that this particular business involved him too.

He had been in Salerno for fifteen days, fifteen days of solitude and busy thoughts, of conjectures and hindsight, of trying to find faults in the case against him and end that whole tale once and for all. Missing his home and children, he spent most of that time alone, not talking to anyone. He'd often found himself in a corner of the cell, crouched over with eyes swollen from crying.

Where was Oreste the braggart, the happy and expansive *guappo*, the arrogant and loud but also kind man (at times, anyway)? Where was the man who always knew what he was doing even when what he was doing was stupid and foolish?

More and more his mind had kept dissociating from reality, to the point that the guards had started using their batons to make him stand straight or to get an answer out of him during roll call. He'd be lost in thinking about Diomira, about the kids, about his job, even the animals, and sometimes the money. How could that poor woman make it on her own, with seven children, the eldest only fifteen? What about legal costs? He and Enrico had splurged on the best of the best in Salerno, the most notable lawyer – and therefore the most expensive – in a burst of confidence and lack of foresight. Only the best for Oreste Solimeno!

Who better than Clemente Mauro esquire, member of parliament for the XXV and XXVI governments of the Kingdom of Italy. Mauro's practice involved many notable lawyers, all very aware of their status and position, a fact fully reflected in their clients' bills. Their meetings and discussions always took place weekly, around some of the best tables of the best Salerno restaurants; the meals themselves were paid for by the only person invited who had no hint of the law, Enrico Solimeno.

But the money was provided by Diomira, who often had to bring it by hand to her brother-in-law, waiting outside the establishment, hungry and tired from the journey.

She could see them through the curtains, talking out loud and laughing, joking with each other. Enrico was often laughing along too, and she never heard her husband's name. Three or four hours later, Enrico would step outside, full of wine and smoke, smirking under his moustache.

"All good Diomira, all good! They're solving everything. A few more days and we're in for a surprise. Mauro is the best lawyer in Salerno – only the best for my brother!"

Diomira would've liked to hear more than just Enrico's word. She wanted to know the details, the actual developments in the case, if Oreste was doing well, and if he was eating. All the things that Enrico seemed not to care about, or at least, seemed not to think about informing her.

Maybe he thought her too ignorant to understand legal proceeding; maybe her position as a woman meant she had to wait in silence, in her place, for things to be steered by her betters: men,

men who did and undid. They started wars and provoked the tears and blood and pain of mothers and wives. They toiled to amass wealth; they killed if they saw it fit, and even if they didn't. Desire for power allowed everything and anything to happen, even murder, even if the consequences spilled over to the women. She knew it would be the same this time, for her, too. Oreste was innocent; she knew that, but those who did the crime were also men.

Men who had a mother or a wife made to suffer for their son or husband and their choice to be "a man" one last time.

CHAPTER 14

Gaetano Cifuni walked, as always, with his side against the wall of the yard. He had never abandoned his habit of always keeping one side covered, looking behind him and casting glances to all sides as much as possible. He never allowed himself to relax or wind down.

This was a result both of a life on the run and a side of paranoia. Especially now, he had nothing to be afraid of; the deal had gone down; he was about to get out.

He cast another glance behind him, hoping for the big show that had been set up for those final hours would start soon, and that he could deal with his last justice collaboration.

He had to play his last part well, on a stage seemingly for no one, but actually in full view of everyone. He knew that everyone was looking at him, some hoping to slide a blade between his ribs, as the rumour about Cifuni the spy, Cifuni the snitch had spread throughout the Penitentiary, and it hadn't been well received.

It had been Farrese and Mollo's fault, sure, but also *Maresciallo* Mancini's. Did he have to register the payments? Couldn't he have slipped the money over? Did he really need a receipt? In any case, everything would be over soon. He looked back again and saw them approach. Two *carabinieri,* with the shift guard.

"Cifuni!" they called out. "Stop and hands on the wall. Random search."

They were much louder than the distance required, almost as if they were trying to draw everyone's attention.

"*Appuntato*, what have I done? I'm leaving tomorrow; what do you think you'll find?" Cifuni played his part, tried to appear surprised and annoyed at this new imposition.

He also raised his voice, but his attempt was a little stilted, unconvincing. Anyone could tell it was a set up, especially from the grins on the faces of both Cifuni and the guards.

"Spread 'em, Cifuni, and quiet. Until you step out that door, you're ours to do with as we please, and we can search you any time we want."

The *carabinieri* had leaned into their roles and added a couple of kicks to get the legs wide apart. They hurt. Their hands rummaged in his pockets.

"Oh, what's this?" one of them asked, pulling out a piece of folded paper.

That's what you just kicked me for, you bastard, Cifuni thought to himself. He kept quiet as agreed, trying to make the scene more believable.

They dragged him, roughly, to the intake office, where newcomers were processed. They forced him to sit at the last desk at the back.

"Cifuni, sign here and it's all over. Then everyone can go home for lunch." They pointed at a pre-written statement about the search, only missing the time and signature.

Cifuni wrote his name without reading it, as he knew what it said:

The paper found upon me by your excellencies was given to me by inmate Panariello Raffaele, who told me to have received it from inmate Oreste Solimeno. The latter, having heard of my release, had me receive the note destined for his brother once back in Capaccio. Your excellencies, during your search, have anticipated my spontaneous decision of handing over said note, as I have no intention of associating myself with inmate Oreste Solimeno.

Not a regret, no sign of remorse, no hesitation. The fact that such a statement might send someone else to prison for life didn't even cross his mind. This was the plan; this is what he did. All they needed now was for Panariello to confirm, and then there would be two witnesses, indubitable facts, and a definite sentencing of Oreste Solimeno.

Panariello had been brought into the plan due to him being the inmate assigned to toilet duties; he had contacts with all the other inmates. He had had some hesitation, as his reward had amounted to a couple of cigarettes and spare change.

Eventually he had given in. They had convinced him that it would be better for his own sake to agree to Cifuni's version of the events, as sometimes memory complications can become health complications, especially if the bones weren't made to withstand beatings explained by sudden falls.

He wandered through the cells, slight and small, broom in hand and thoughts buzzing in his head, looking to tell anyone the story about the note being entirely made up. Solimeno hadn't given him anything. Solimeno hadn't even spoken to him since his arrival.

He told Mollo; he told Umberto Folle; he told Vinceno Buonanno. But words spoken out loud were one thing; the ones written down in the statement were another, and he had signed those. Whenever his conscience got too loud, the sound of his bones creaking grew louder, a looming threat of what would happen if he spilled everything; then he'd desist.

After being studied by the Director and the Chief Officer of the Penitentiary, the note was sent two days later to *Maresciallo* Mancini in Capaccio.

"Bertolucci! Come here, *appuntato*." Mancini was glowing. The tips of his moustache seemed to rise even higher, an extension of the smile across his entire face.

"We got him! We finally got him: this is proof that Solimeno is as guilty as the devil himself. See? I was right! I was right all along.

Read this." He handed over the note to Bertolucci: it was mostly faded by now, and just barely legible.

"How does this mean we got him?" Bertolucci asked.

"It was taken from Cifuni. Oreste had given it to him via another inmate, knowing Cifuni was about to be released."

"Ah. Cifuni." Bertolucci said nothing else, and he didn't need to. It was obvious that those two words expressed his entire thoughts on the matter. Mancini, on the other hand, seemed utterly convinced.

He read the note:

Dear Agostino, my brother,

I send you my friend, the man carrying this note, and I ask you to go speak immediately with Mauro esquire in Salerno. You will let him know that I am still denying everything and you will advise our brother Alfonso to also deny everything. This messenger will explain the rest. My good wishes to everyone, your brother Oreste. July 7 1922.

Bertolucci tried really hard not to burst out laughing. The message was as fake as a three lira note. The opening alone was enough to give it away. Who would use such a sequence of words, detailing the family relationship and full name? Not even letters from two centuries prior did that. It would either be *dear Agostino* or *dear brother.*

The contents, as much as the prosecution saw it useful for a life sentence, said nothing at all. Especially, they said nothing new to any party. Deny everything meant nothing, and there was no need to tell this to a lawyer – the inmate had access to the lawyer through the Penitentiary any time.

What was the messenger supposed to explain, then? Had they asked Cifuni or Panariello about the contents of the oral message, so secretive to not be allowed in a written note but good enough for two barely known messengers?

Bertolucci stood up.

"With your leave, sir, I would like to go through my papers and Solimeno's one more time," he told Mancini.

"You're still not convinced? Do everything you need to do, *appuntato*. For the sake of justice and our consciences. I will start drafting up my report to the Prosecutor; I will explain the note and everything around it, so he has time to decide into which well to throw the keys to Solimeno's cell."

Bertolucci moved to the other room, pulled out the file, and started rifling through it. The size of the file kept growing by the day, filled with statements, records, and notes.

He was looking for a handwritten note from Oreste but found none. There were a few signatures, on statements – both handwritten and typed up with the new Olivetti M20 from the judge's office – but it was only a signature, not enough to compare. The note didn't even have a signature (would you look at that!) Which meant he had to pay a visit to Solimeno's place.

He would've preferred avoiding doing so, as understandably those folks started panicking for the last few months whenever a *carabiniere* showed up.

He had to, however. He left the barracks, cap on his head, not caring for the July heat, and set off for the uphill road to the Solimeno home, just outside Capaccio.

CHAPTER 15

Time in summer was set by work in the fields.

Between the start of June and the start of July, people harvested wheat with long sickles sharpened with whetstones. Many bodies were needed to complete the task, and people worked with neighbours and friends across a number of farms and fields.

Wearing three finger protectors made of reeds, the *cannilli,* one hand would hold the bundle of wheat. Each bundle cut, the wheat was left on the ground for the younger kids to pick up into a pile, kids of many age groups, cousins, friends, siblings, fighting and laughing with each other, everyone having a good time.

When sunset marked the end of the long day of work, which started at dawn, everyone would share a meal together not far from the bales. Tired faces, smiling faces, from a job well done for the adults and the blissful ignorance of the children.

A couple of weeks after the harvest, the threshing started, which required twenty people or more, and so neighbours and friends were brought in again. The oxen pulled the machines (steam threshers) from home to home, and four labourers with wooden forks threw the bales into the machine, and a woman picked up the grains. Two more women were tasked with cutting the bales open, placing themselves on either side of the input slot for the machine. Inside the thresher, three men oversaw the bags of wheat. The whole task also required four workers above, and one below to drive the machine; another five were needed for loading hay from the machine to the hay pile. The husk pile itself required two workers up top, while two others loaded the husks prepared by a pair of workers with rakes.

At the start and the end of each threshing, the steam machine let out a long whistle, calling everyone to gather round and to warn the next house, for the lead farmer to head out with their beasts to pick up the machine.

It was, in short, a job that required collaboration and synergy from all family members, cousins, and friends, a job that without that collaboration would mean going hungry.

For the Solimeno family, all of this had been tradition up to the previous year. Though already numerous, they also required friends and neighbours to help with the field work. That year, however, they had been left alone.

What Mayor Lombardi's speech had suggested during the funeral had been taken literally by the people of Capaccio. Those guilty of the slaughter had to be ostracized, their families left to their own.

As the circle kept getting tighter around Oreste, friends lessened in number; acquaintances seemed to forget about them, and even family started moving away, as if one's sins could taint the entire kin, even the children.

For this reason, when Bertolucci appeared in the yard outside Diomira's home, he found only two young girls sweeping the ground with brooms much bigger than them.

Filomena and Caterina were Oreste's eldest daughters, the two who were dealing with his incarceration the worst. Filomena was fifteen by now and was a woman by the standards of the time – except for the fact that the psychological stress and trauma from the ordeal had meant that she had actually regressed to a pre-pubescent state and would remain such for life. Another victim of the Filette events, really.

She raised her head just enough to see the red stripes on the *appuntato*'s pant leg, and her blood froze in her veins. She said nothing, but she gestured with her head to Caterina, who ran back inside.

"Filomena, don't worry. I'm only here to talk to your mom and bring her news of your dad." Bertolucci knew the name of each of the Solimeno children and had no difficulty telling who she was despite never having met her personally.

Filomena seemed surprised at her name being known.

"Mom is inside," she said, then fell quiet again, waiting for him to speak instead.

"Your dad is doing well, you know," Bertolucci smiled at her. "He sends his best wishes to you and your siblings. Can you call your mother out here, so I can let her know, too?"

Dressed in black as if in mourning and with a black band holding back her hair, Diomira, who had been warned by Caterina, appeared at the door. She was thirty-eight years old but at the moment looked at least sixty.

He saw her and moved closer. "Good morning," he said. "My name is *appuntato* Bertolucci, and I have a few questions for you." He didn't wait for a reply and immediately added: "Do you happen to have any document or letter signed by your husband, inside? I am not looking for evidence against him, don't worry – in fact, exactly the opposite. I would like to help Oreste. I think he's innocent."

Diomira studied him for some time and must have decided he was sincere. She said nothing, took him by his hand, and pulled him inside, directly to the bedroom and the ebony desk that was clearly more valuable than all the other pieces of furniture in the house. She opened a drawer and pulled out a bundle of papers held together with string.

"Here," she said. "These are all the papers we have in the house. I cannot read, so I cannot tell you if they are Oreste's or someone else's. You can look through them all."

There were contract copies, invoices, a few letters for Oreste, the sentence from the Arbitrary Commission. Nothing he had written, which made sense; letters are sent once written. Received letters are kept. But nothing? Nothing at all?

He handed her back the bundle and had a sudden realization.

"Diomira, what's happening with the workshop in town? Who's running the place at the moment?"

"No one. We shut it down when Oreste was taken away. All the food we took home. We handed shoes that needed repairing back to customers; then we locked the door, and no one has been since. I don't think we would have done much even if we had kept it open – everyone avoids us now."

"May I go take a look?"

Diomira did not reply, but she opened another drawer and took out a key. She handed it over to Bertolucci, who took it. He curtly nodded, and headed straight back to the door, towards town. He was barely halfway through the yard when he heard her calling to him. "*Appuntato*," she said, tears in her voice. "Thank you."

The key turned in the lock with a creaking sound, and the pungent smell of dust hit Bertolucci's nostrils as soon as he opened the door. It was dark inside, but he knew where to look. He had seen, every time he'd walked past the workshop, the credit lists posted in the window, when Oreste wanted to publicly remind his debtors of how much they owed.

He was looking for the notebook, the ledger made out of bread wrapping paper tied up with string.

He found it, almost immediately, placed on a shelf now empty of its original contents. It had names, numbers, notes, all penned by Oreste Solimeno. Enough to compare to the requisitioned note, which he was pretty sure was a different pen entirely.

Mancini was not in the office.

Bertolucci waited for him for hours, wanting to show him immediately what he thought would exonerate Oreste Solimeno. He also knew he wouldn't be able to convince his superior officer, no matter how much proof he'd provide.

He read through the entire Solimeno file as he waited, but found nothing he didn't already know by now. He stood up from his desk and peeked into Mancini's office. He could see his superior officer's hat on the rack, but he was nowhere to be seen. He wouldn't be seen for the rest of the night either: the hat was a sign that Mancini had slipped into his civilian clothes, probably to go drink at Raffaele's tavern.

CHAPTER 16

The dim light of the oil lamps peering out of the windows of the old houses barely lit up the narrow streets of Capaccio.

Ten years prior, the zeal and ingenuity of a young engineer by the name of Migliacci, Capaccio had received its first electricity lines. The work, however, had slowed down and other than a couple private homes and the Cirio factory, very few actually made use of it. Public illumination was scarce and insufficient, and still used acetylene lamps.

Darkness easily spread through the nooks of each street, and walking on the rough streets was even rougher than during daytime.

Mancini, after leaving the tavern, had started down one of these streets, along with his thoughts currently dipped in wine. He wasn't a big drinker, and Raffaele's wine – fresh and a little strong – had gone straight to his head, though the fact had not stopped him from having more. The feeling, overall, was pleasant.

Wine is great, Mancini thought. *It lessens pain and lightens the mood.* He finally felt like that damn investigation was finally at a crucial point, maybe even a decisive one. He had known, from the start, that Oreste Solimeno had been involved in the massacre of Filette. Now he had enough evidence to prove it.

Under the influence, what Mancini was not considering in his logic, was that the evidence had been gathered not via a proper investigation, but rather via tricks and subterfuge, some of which he had orchestrated himself, to ensure that reality fit the idea he had formed about it out of his preconceived notions.

This was one the more common mistakes for any investigator. Adapting the world to their convictions and intuitions, shaping data and facts from investigations rather than letting the latter influence and contribute to the former. The additional layer of having done so intentionally, then, is the tipping point between investigator and executioner, between man of law and criminal.

Mancini, this time, did not care. He was certain Oreste was guilty, and any means justified the end. He owed it to the children, slaughtered so barbarically, to Rosario and Pasqualina; he owed it to lovely Caterina, so horribly disfigured.

He caught himself thinking fondly of Caterina, of her shapely legs, and grew irritated with himself. He forced the thoughts away, ascribing them to the influence of the wine. He was getting good at this exercise in conscience cleansing.

He turned into the next dark alley and almost stumbled into Enrico Solimeno, their noses almost touching.

He's going to knife me. Everything is going to be over. I'm done for. He was so calm as this new thought formed in his mind.

Despite having all the reasons to be, he wasn't afraid, maybe due to the alcohol: it was dark; they were alone; no one had seen them; he was impaired by the wine. He wasn't afraid, but he still took a step back, instinctively, the better to look at the other man.

Enrico's usual smirk, under his moustache, was not present at this time; instead, his features clearly showed the same shock as Mancini and confirmed that this had been an entirely fortuitous meeting for them both.

Nonetheless, Enrico was sober, a large man, and fully aware of the situation. He stared at the *maresciallo*, squaring him up, his gaze turning to distaste and loathing. He could have; this was the right opportunity. He could've struck the man on the spot and left him to die. He would've fixed his brother's problems, and much faster than the professional lawyer: removing the main accuser, the lead investigator, and party most invested in Oreste's sentencing to the gallows. The whole investigation would fold; evidence would no longer be considered, and everything would settle again.

Mancini – as the adrenaline had swiftly sobered him up – had come to the same conclusion and was expecting Enrico to strike any moment now.

Instead, Enrico Solimeno – head of the family this inch the side of being *camorristi*, the unrivalled *guappo* of Capaccio, the man who had slapped a judge in full daylight – raised his hat and simply said: "Good evening, *maresciallo*."

"A good evening to you," Mancini replied, even more surprised and entirely disarmed by the greeting, worse than if he'd been shot.

The pallor of his face, barely lit by the dim light through a window, jarred with the darkness of the alley, and a bead of sweat started crawling down his cheek.

"Fear not, Mancini. I am no killer," Enrico continued. "And neither is my brother Oreste. You are forcing him to rot in that cell, away from his family and his home, and by doing so you are going against the laws you claim to apply and enforce. I do not know if you will be held accountable before justice of men, but I do know you will have to answer for it before your conscience if not a higher power."

Mancini didn't reply, in case any word from him might change the other man's intentions. In fact, he stepped to one side, offering the right side of the street as knights in the 1500s used to do. He sped up, left Enrico behind, and headed straight for the barracks.

He never looked back until he could see the door and felt his breathing slow again and fear slip into exhaustion and relief.

Bertolucci had long left by that point, and the two only met again in the morning.

The *appuntato* arrived earlier than his usual, and waited in front of Mancini's door, with Oreste's papers under one arm and the impatience of sharing his news on his mind.

Mancini arrived much more slowly, refreshed and with a spring in his step, as if he had only witnessed the events of the previous night, rather than being their protagonist.

He had slept off the alcohol and regained all of his assuredness. He had also gained some additional cockiness, it seemed. He spoke to Bertolucci with a sunny disposition that was unlike him.

"*Appuntato*! Good morning! You were waiting for me? Come in, come in."

"Good morning, sir," Bertolucci replied and immediately jumped into what he intended to say. "Look at what I found in Solimeno's workshop yesterday. Lists, written by Oreste himself. And this, this is the note from the Penitentiary. Look at the handwriting: it doesn't match, at all."

He had not sat down, simply unloaded and unrolled the papers onto Mancini's desk, covering it almost entirely.

Mancini did not lose his smile. He picked up the note, folded it, and placed it into his breast pocket. He then turned to look at the lists and invoices, and his smile turned into raucous laughter.

"Bertolucci, my friend – baking paper! Do you want us to offer the judge some of our breakfast? Shopping lists! Anyone could have written these! You want them to become official papers in the investigation? Go to the other room; get some stamps; let's notarize them! Or go see if Stormillo, the notary, is free today, maybe."

"Sir, you know perfectly well that Oreste would post these in his window. You've seen them yourself, countless times. Also, how many apothecaries and cobblers who can read and write are there in Capaccio? Even counting all notables and notaries, I can still list by name everyone who can write."

"What I know perfectly well, *appuntato*, is that there are witnesses, eye-witnesses, who have stated that Oreste Solimeno took part in the slaughter. There are incontrovertible facts that prove that he had motive for Rosario De Nicola to disappear from the face of the Earth. What I *know* is that he tried escaping these barracks, and that you! You caught him. What I *know* is that our colleagues in Salerno have requisitioned a note which is effectively a confession, and the person they found it on was given it by Oreste Solimeno. What I *don't* know is of anyone, any single person, who remembers where Oreste was on the day of the massacre. I don't know of any alibis or evidence to the contrary. Listen, Bertolucci: Oreste Solimeno is guilty. I know, deep in my conscience, that he is as guilty as a devil and if – if – we resorted to a couple of tricks, we did so to ensure that justice is served."

CHAPTER 17

Alone and avoiding all conversations with anyone, he had spent the last two years as an outcast among the outcast. He had tried setting himself apart from the other inmates, as he truly believed he had nothing in common with any of them. This had led him to spiral into loneliness, and to the brink of folly.

He had never seen a Van Gogh painting, and he probably ignored the artist's existence entirely, but if he had ever come across the *Prisoners' Round* he would have recognized a snapshot of his own existence: everyone walking in a circle, in humiliation and disappointment, in a courtyard surrounded by tall walls, and a single person – himself, Oreste – stepping out of the line with the hope of flying above, beyond, elsewhere, as the two small butterflies, uncaring for human limitations.

The date of the trial had arrived. Oreste had reached it entirely alone and jaded, his mind starting to crack, alternating between pure euphoria and speeches against the authorities, screeds against the guards and anyone coming closer, and days of utter apathy and despair, shutting down, closing himself off more and more.

He had barely seen his own lawyers, and even less so Mauro esquire; his family visits had also dwindled, and he hadn't heard from home in three months.

The gears of the justice system, on the other hand, had kept turning. The trial was ready, the defence – though he had little faith in them – had also moved precisely and professionally, among papers and people finding evidence of his innocence.

The times, however, had changed.

The new regime, a government that relied on the finality of punishment and making examples for the sake of justice, a government that relied on punishing one to teach a hundred, would never allow for a series of events such as the slaughter of the De Nicola to go without a culprit. The two actual killers were still at large, and one was even unnamed. The only person available, and in the hands of justice, was the instigator – punishment had to be dealt.

The courts, going against their supposed impartiality and adherence to the law, were settling into this new line of justice, the black of the gowns indistinguishable from the black of the shirts.

On October 10th, 1925, after two hours of well-received eloquence proving he was still the best in the Salerno system, the lawyer for the defence Clemente Mauro, member of parliament until the previous government, and chair of the board including the lawyers Arturo De Felice, Guido Vestuti and Vincenzo Farina, was reaching his conclusion. He had shown the negligent work of the investigation and the lack of tangible proof, the entirely summarized case brought before the court, and the lack of a true motive for his client.

Mauro – tired from the political events that had taken place in the past year, leading to his downfall before the new masters, and from his age and health – moved slowly between the bar and the court. He felt, nonetheless, at home, pacing the room that had seen him play the main part for so many years: chin raised, gaze proud, thumbs on either side of his chest, tucked into the gown.

He accompanied his words with small gestures, as if to underline how he did not require theatrics to make his points, only masterful pauses, silences, increased volume, and whispers.

He had everyone, even the Public Prosecutor, hanging on his every word.

"We do not wish to continue, at this point, and add to the sizable volume of the notes of the defence, lest we incur the tedium of those listening. We could have noted the increased efforts around the witnesses, encouraged to proffer statements which include details of the absurd and the unbelievable, only to be contradicted by other witnesses; we have preferred not to indulge in such an exercise, leaving such a task to the evidence examined by the magistrates of the prosecution.

The investigation shows a significant void and several instances of negligence. Filling the former, perhaps, and removing the latter may make the truth reveal itself.

If there are doubts still remaining, even before we plead the court for the absolution of Oreste Solimeno, then we ask that a follow-up investigation is performed first. Specifically, so that we may determine the motives and alibi of our client.

We believe, however, that such a course will not be necessary.

It is said that the Council of Ten, which controlled the fate of the ancient Venetian Republic and its courts, would never consider accusations that were not upheld by at least two witnesses, or that revealed themselves unfounded on first study. And those were dark times, during which people still were kept as slaves.

Today, we have come so far; all citizens are allowed to live freely through the day, every day. Today, justice represents the highest social function, and as such, we denounce the artifice, the slander, the lies, the subterfuges required to strike at an innocent man, a hard worker and a father.

Let us hope, then, that we can once again see the triumph of truth and justice.

Both call for recognizing the innocence of Oreste Solimeno."

The ovation that would have followed such a conclusion, spontaneously, as that was the case for each remark delivered by Mauro in his Salerno, this time was barely welcomed with a timid applause, some mumbling, and a strange silence to follow.

Mauro was a little shocked at the reaction, remembering the unconditional adoration he had been used to, and despite the expression of the President and Judge of the court during his speech giving him a different indication, he realized that this trial specifically had already been decided. Long before his work, no matter what clause, what paper, what witness he might have brought, nothing would have changed the Court's opinion: Oreste would be sentenced, and his sentence would serve as an example.

Barely two hours later in the Council chambers – the time required literally to write down the sentence – in the name of His Majesty Vittorio Emanuele III, by the Grace of God and the will of the Nation, King of Italy, the President of the Ordinary Court of Salerno Sir Vincenzo Spagnuolo esquire, with the intervention of Public Prosecution represented by Sir Giovanni Di Muro, Assistant General Attorney, Oreste Solimenò, cobbler from Capaccio was found guilty and sentenced to prison for life.

The judge's words were muffled in Oreste's ears, as if spoken from a great distance, though he was barely three metres from the President's seat, behind a square cage as was customary with defendants already in custody.

He had followed the entire trial as a spectator, or so he felt, even bored with the proceedings. Hoping to see a friend, a member of his family, Diomira, or any of his brothers, he kept shifting his gaze across the room. Not the children. He knew they would be allowed into the court. How would Diomira, his dearest Diomoira, be able to make it anyway? Who would tell her about the date of the trial? No one told him anything until the day itself, and all of the lawyers of his defence had not spoken to him in months.

Still, he hoped he could spot Enrico, or maybe Alfonso, or even Agostino. They had all reduced the frequency of their visits, even of their letters, as if they no longer truly cared about his fate. With the same reckless indifference when he had heard the sentence, he was now processing the fact that he might die alone, maybe not soon, but definitely alone.

He had understood the sentence perfectly, despite the pompous and legal jargon, including the corollary consequences of the main part: no public office, no legal recourse, removal of parental rights, marital rights, and prohibition of drafting a will, including invalidation of the will made before the sentence.

They had decided he no longer had a wife, no longer had children, no longer was a person.

With the resignation of those who know that everything is lost, he offered his wrists to the guard who had come to escort him on the short trip from the Tribunal to the prisoner transport car. He watched the last scene of a life without walls disappear behind the misty eyes of tears.

CHAPTER 18

A life sentence, a way to describe prison for the rest of a person's life, also used to mean – in the original Italian *ergastolo* – the location in which said sentence would be lived out. The Ancient Greek word is commonly translated as "work house" but *ergastoli* were very much prisons, often high security ones, exclusively for incarceration. All human rights were discarded, and each sentenced within would lose his dignity before losing, inevitably, his life.

Among all of the *ergastoli* across Italy, almost all built upon islands, one of the most notable not for its location but rather for the amount of morbid tales about it, was the Santo Stefano Correctional Facility in the Pontine Islands.

Oreste Solimeno was transferred from Salerno, along with four others from who knows where, gathered at the port in Naples, and they all arrived at night.

The central tower cast two beams, lighting up the three cell wings arranged in a circle around it, as a theatre – a panopticon, even. Oreste, still stunned from the journey, watched that fascinating construction with the awe of a tourist before the Coliseum, unaware of the heavy bars beyond the red bricks, separating the real world from the inmates.

He was assigned to a single cell, as his sentence also included nightly isolation, and he immediately experienced the hygiene elements which would undoubtedly send him to the next life much faster. Cockroaches, beetles, bugs crawling freely across the floor, and small piles of mouse excrement in the corners – the real citizens of Santo Stefano were vermin and pests.

Isolation wasn't what weighed upon him; even during the day, when he had the chance to talk to the other inmates, he preferred to stay alone, focusing on his chores, avoiding comments and cliques as he still felt he had nothing in common with those criminals. He was innocent, a victim of a conspiracy.

Was he? What had he told Calabrese that day, almost nine years ago? Had he really suggested that he organize and carry out the murders? He had convinced himself, in time, that he had not, he could not. He did talk to the killers, sure, many times. He had convinced them of his status as a *camorrista*, someone with the power of life and death over others, and that there had been more than one reason for him to have it in for the De Nicola family. He did not remember, however, to have told that criminal beast, that devil made man, to go over there and kill them all. Calabrese had done everything by himself, and as is often the case, the real guilty usually get away with it, and justice needed someone to pay for the crime.

These were the thoughts that regularly ebbed and flowed in his mind, distracting him from his tasks and causing a heavy reminder from the guard's baton. Even so, the worst of their treatment was not reserved for him, or for other regular criminals – everyone had started considering him just not quite all there, not that it meant they spared him from their reminders.

The guards' attention, their more ruthless attention, was devoted to the political prisoners, the enemies of the new regime, sent there by the special courts: communists, socialists, dissidents of all colours.

These prisoners initially had their own section, a recess with darker and filthier cells, if that were possible, and their own little sign on the cell door: *WARNING – Dangerous Prisoner.*

As time moved on, however, their number increased and it had become impossible to keep them all to one section, and becoming cell neighbours, they all mingled and shared spaces with the regular inmates during daily chores.

During their breaks, Oreste would watch them, emaciated but proud, gathering in huddles that the guards swiftly dispersed, as they were forbidden from gathering in numbers bigger than three. Despite the prohibitions and the accompanying beatings, the huddles still formed, sometimes with another seven or eight inmates.

Their charisma was undeniable, no matter one's ideology or political leanings, and Oreste – who was most definitely not a socialist, and in fact supported many aspects of the Fascist government (despite the role it had had in his sentence) – was drawn to them. Straining his ear to catch conversations and discussions, he caught himself paying attention to the diminutive figure of one Sandro Pertini.

Pertini would talk in a low volume and would always warn others swiftly if the guards moved closer, batons at the ready. Another of the group, on the other hand, would frequently linger and even berate the guards, resulting in a heavier beating than most others, every time.

They had targeted him from the very first day: a young, restless man from Calabria, who seemed to become more rooted in his beliefs the more beatings he took. The more they beat him, the more upright he walked, and the louder he shouted in their faces, with all the force of his political activism and education.

His name was Rocco Pugliese, born on January 27th 1903 in Palmi, close to Reggio Calabria, and a member since a young age of the Socialist Party. He had then founded, with others, the Palmi branch of the Italian Communist Party in 1921, becoming its secretary at eighteen years of age.

Palmi was a stronghold of the left and a frequent target of the fascist violence of militia and sympathizers, as their branch had also been founded at the same time. Their clashes escalated and reached a climax in the summer of 1925, during patron saint celebration. The partying crowds, the heat, and the accumulated tensions of years had resulted in the death of a *black shirt,* a fascist militant, and unleashed political repercussions via a special court, sentencing several communists to incarceration for life throughout the country. Rocco Pugliese had ended up in Santo Stefano, the worst *ergastolo* of them all.

Pugliese's cell, due to the overpopulation of the facility, was not in the political prisoner section, but rather in the general population area, directly across from where Oreste Solimeno had spent his last five years. Oreste had exchanged a few words but kept mostly to himself until one evening in October, where he found himself having a pleasant conversation with the young man.

They did not speak of parties, or politics, or the reasons for them being in the same place, but instead of their families, their faded memories of home, and they fantasized about a future beyond these walls.

Oreste had warmed up to him, and when curfew fell, he lay upon his filthy cot with a smile he had lacked in years, promising to pick up where they left off as soon as he could.

CHAPTER 19

"Mamma! Mamma!"

He heard the words muffled, but clear. He wasn't sure if he was dreaming them, but he opened his eyes and tried to focus beyond his cell. More dull thuds, like a carpet being beaten, and muffled cries.

He stood up, hobbled in the darkness of his cell to the bars, to find out the source of the sounds. The cells were not directly facing each other, but at an angle – and yet, Oreste strained his sight towards Rocco Pugliese's cell, and he saw everything.

There were four of them, wielding heavy metal bars, half a metre long and half the size of a wrist. They had immobilized Rocco, tied his hands behind his back with a ripped-up bedsheet, another part of which was shoved down his throat to muffle his screams. With a blanket over his head to block all vision and increase the fear, they were engaged in what was known as *Sant'Antonio*. The name came from a *camorra* practice, a punitive visit, and involved a severe beating to cause broken bones and bruises all over.

But Rocco was not taking it. Even the four guards were having issues trying to hold him down, and the bars started flailing, striking more violently upon limbs and back. A few hits came point-first, to the stomach, to the groin, and despite the gag, Oreste could clearly make out the grunts of pain which would have been screams. The blanket around his head only barely lessened the blows to the head, but a few struck the naked body, and Oreste flinched at the second-hand pain.

One of the guards stomped with his steel boots and kicked Rocco right between the legs. The young man folded onto himself and lowered his head right as another guard was bringing down a steel bar. He might have been aiming for his chest, or to crack a rib, but instead made contact with a temple, and everything suddenly fell silent and still.

The four killers looked at each other, with clear disappointment at the fun ending so soon and a visible lack of remorse. Without speaking, according to whatever plan they had arranged, they removed the blanket from Rocco's head, untied his wrists, and using the same sheet, made a noose and placed it around his neck. They hung him from the highest bar on the window, removed the gag, and left the cell one by one, slipping back into the dark hallway.

The one at the back, who looked like he was in charge, lingered at the door before locking it again, three turns of a large key. Who knows how many such beatings had taken place in that spot. He turned to head for the hallway, and his gaze met the shocked face of Oreste Solimeno.

He had been leaning against his own cell bars, holding onto them, his eyes wide with horror, drinking in the morbid spectacle. He saw the guard; the guard saw him, and neither spoke. Oreste knew that it would be better for him to have gone back to sleep, or at least to pretend as much, but his instincts had brought him to watch. He looked again at the guard and spotted a tight smile on the man's face – an even greater horror than the scene he had just witnessed.

"Solimeno saw," the guard was standing in front of the director's desk, cap in hand, and the pained expression of someone being caught, rather than remorse for a beating turned murder.

"Solimeno? Who is Solimeno?"

Achille Morandi, Director of the Santo Stefano Correctional Facility, barely looked up from his paperwork. He moved very little and ate a lot – he was a large man, wedged between the chair's armrests, trapped in it almost as his inmates were trapped in his facility. Beyond the walls were only sea and rocks; his cell was the island itself, a little larger than that of others, but a cell nonetheless.

There was a reason for Morandi not to leave that place, where society, the real world and real life were but a distant memory: it was filled with men. Many men, some young and beautiful, and he loved each and every one of them. He could watch them shower; he could watch them topless, sweating during summer chores, chest glinting in the sun; he could talk to them; he could touch them, because he was the law in that place.

He knew that the regime knew about him, about his orientation. The government abhorred everything that was not macho masculinity, but also knew that several of its key officers were gay men, and everyone knew about everyone else. As long as they tolerated each other, ignoring the violence and abuse of fascism, covering up thefts and rumours, enabling the hunger for power of the lowest black shirt, the exchange allowed them to survive.

Which meant that now, the issue was not to report the death of Rocco Pugliese, and not to punish his murderers. He so wanted to punish those guards for what they had done to that lovely young man. He had set himself a limit, and he would not mingle with the political prisoners, but he had spotted that man since he first stepped in here.

But the more pressing issue was the existence of a witness, this Solimeno, whose name meant nothing to him. He couldn't have been young or attractive, or he would've remembered.

"Who is Solimeno?"

"His first name is Oreste. He's from Salerno, I believe, or around there. He was sentenced for slaughtering women and children. He was the instigator. Something about family feuds; he's been screaming about his innocence since he got here five years ago. They all do."

"Oh, yes! I remember him now. The children, the killings." The director tried reorganizing his thoughts and all the stories he had read about his guests. It was hard to keep track of all of them; there were so many, and especially hard if they weren't quite his type either, to put a face to a name, no matter how heinous the crime.

"What's he like?" he asked. "Politically, I mean."

"He has never shown any dissent or unrest. In fact, he has often spoken fondly of the government and the *Duce.* Nothing specific, and he's not quite all there. He's introverted, prefers to be alone; everyone thinks he's lost his mind, though that also comes as no surprise in here."

"Very well. If everyone says he's lost his mind, then he's lost it. We can't keep him here; the mad see things that aren't true all the time, like a particularly heavy beating or someone being killed when it's clear that the only deaths here are by suicide or natural causes."

The guard smiled. "I'll have the papers drawn up, then?"

"Yes, we're sending him to Aversa."

CHAPTER 20

From the summary report of the
DIRECTOR OF THE JUDICIAL ASYLUM OF AVERSA

Mod. 343 M

Inmate SOLIMENO Oreste, parents Antonio and Filomena Iannelli, born in Capaccio (Salerno) on 1st August 1883, of poor extraction, occupation cobbler, married, was admitted to this institute on 30th October 1930 from the Santo Stefano facility as a life-sentence inmate due to multiple homicide.

Personal history reveals he belonged to a family of questionable reputation and with a history of alcohol abuse.

The subject proved irascible and impulsive in childhood, enjoyed gambling and wine later in life, and revealed himself negligent in his work and not ethical in societal living.

Since his first day in this institute, he has manifested psychopathic symptoms of mental confusion, with ideation and sensorial misattributions, integrating the initial assessment of the condition known as carceral psychosis, not uncommon in inmates who experience isolation. The syndrome, thanks to the appropriate therapy, has decreased in severity and after eight months of convalescence, has regressed entirely. The patient appears entirely reintegrated in his original psychic conditions.

Thus, the subject is dismissed from this institute on 2nd March 1932.

Aversa, 20th April 1932 X E F
Director
Filippo Saporito

The letter was signed by professor Filippo Saporito, a luminary of psychiatry, and fully explained that Oreste was perfectly sane. However, it never found its way to who should have arranged the transfer back to Santo Stefano, and instead Oreste was transported to the Judicial Asylum of Reggio Emilia, where he would spend the rest of his days.

The few lines that Saporito had written in Aversa summarized the entirety of Oreste's life, and effectively meant: you sent me a man who was accused of multiple murders, but was definitely nowhere near insane; you locked him up in isolation and solitary confinement, and I'd be surprised if he didn't develop some form of delusion as a result, to the point that his condition cleared barely eight months later despite this place not being Heaven on Earth, and the patient met several actual insane people while here; that said, he was not mad before he came here, and he is not mad now, so please take him back.

The priorities of those interested in the events, of course, were not to determine whether Oreste was unwell, but rather that he be unable to testify what he had seen happen to poor Rocco Pugliese. Despite the year and a half since the young communist's death, it would have been better for the sole witness not to return to the same penitentiary, unless a second murder immediately took place to cover the first.

No, whoever had power over the situation considered it less risky to send him instead to another location, an asylum; no matter what he might say, among all the various delusions and deliriums, his testimony would account to nothing.

And so, ten years after the massacre in Filette, Oreste Solimeno found himself sentenced once more for life, in yet another prison, this time on land but even further from his family. A family which had stumbled down the social ladder so utterly to have found themselves back on the bottom rung.

Family ties had weakened; the multiple streams of cousinhood that previously flowed into the Solimeno river and made its core strength and network, had suddenly dried up, leaving Diomira and the children entirely to themselves.

The closer kin, those brothers who had initially also found themselves involved in the case – Enrico, Agostino, Alfonso – had also started distancing themselves, returning to their regular lives.

Selling the last of their belongings and property, and trying to raise the children without any help, Diomira tried where she could to make ends meet. The youngest – Saverio, Ermelindo, and Tecla – had been taken in by the Papal Orphanage of the Holy Virgin in Pompeii; Canio took on as many jobs as he could in the mornings and tried going through primary school in the evenings.

The eldest had started taking their own paths: Antonio had started his own "business" and made up for his lack of education with the will of his twenty-three years of age and his farmer cunning. He had handed back his book to his mother, who had traded it for her copper pot, and asked her to retrieve the kitchen tool as "the paper wasn't good enough to cook in" and he'd have no more use for it.

Filomena and Caterina, on the other hand, had married. The weddings hadn't been anything special, nor had they been with high-ranking or status men, of course – who would marry the daughters of a man sentenced to life, if not young men without even the eyes to cry, as local sayings claimed? Vincenzo Trippa, a hunter, and Pasquale Dello Schiavo, cow herder, respectively. They also hadn't really bettered their hunger or their status, only getting worse with each generation on either side.

The children, despite it all, despite the rumours and the mocking, the murmurs and the whispering, despite the ostracizing that authorities had set up and the people had happily enforced, grew proud of their name, proud of being Oreste Solimeno's children, and proud to claim they still supported his innocence.

They missed him, dearly, and they had definitely romanticized their memories of him from before the events, adding enough flourishes to make him more of a story than a man.

Thanks to Diomira, they'd bring up stories from their very early childhoods, which none of them would be able to remember. It had been too long, and it was uncertain if those moments had ever actually taken place.

And so, for Tecla and Ermelinda, Oreste was dear old daddy, all affection and love, who would come tired from work in the evenings, but always with a smile on his face. He would lift them up onto his lap, and he'd always have a piece of fruit or candy and kiss them all on their heads before dining together.

The two girls wrote down all of those moments twice a year, for Christmas and Easter, when they wrote their letters from the orphanage in Pompei, as the nuns demanded. They felt lucky, despite everything, to be able to write letters to their dad, even if he was imprisoned and so far away, as most of their friends had no parents to speak of at all. An orphanage is still an orphanage however, despite the education and the three meals a day, and it still has its walls, its rules, and its fences.

Tall fences, made with barbed wire, dividing the wings for boys and those for girls. Saverio and Tecla, despite living so close to each other, spent most of the time the genders were both allowed in the courtyard, reaching through the fencing, squeezing each other's hands, almost as a game.

They did not tell their dad about this in their letters. Everyone was fine; everything was swell; the future would be even better if God would allow them to all be together again.

All the letters, the postcards, the parcels regularly arrived in Reggio Emilia, at the asylum. They never reached Oreste.

They had been ordered to keep the patient free from outside stimuli; he was not allowed to remember the outside or his past life, nor was he allowed any contact with the outside, lest he develop more of a syndrome about his condition on the inside.

With time, blurring the sights, smells, and names of whatever might bring him back to Tempone square, looking down upon the green fields and the distant blue of the sea, Oreste closed himself off personally, in an effort to forget the past and the real world.

In the cold of winter and the sticky heat of Reggio Emilia summers, in the middle of actual insane patients who would scream and bite and strike at each other, much like outside people would strike and kill in the name of this or that ideology in a war that almost annihilated humanity itself; separated from all this by a heavy door of wood and iron, half an arm thick, Oreste Solimeno spent a day after another between four walls that were once white, unaware of what was happening in Italy, and forgot what had happened to him at all.

CHAPTER 21

Dark, then light.

Dim at first, then flashes of bright light.

A large, fully set table at the centre of an enormous room in a house he has never seen before, but he knows is his. He has built it, at last, on the hill above Capaccio.

It's a housewarming lunch; everyone's here: siblings, children, nieces, and nephews. The children have their own side of the table, all the children, including friends and family. He doesn't know them all, but they make him happy.

Oh! He does know who they are: they are the children of Rosario De Nicola, who is sitting next to him. He's chatting with him, with the complicit smile of an old friend, as if they'd just sealed a deal. And it must have been a good deal too, because Rosario arranges piles of notes on the table.

There's so much money. He doesn't need to count it, because he knows exactly how much is in there: thirty-thousand liras. His life is looking up, finally: a new house, cash, a family prosperous in children and kin, the respect of the other people in Capaccio.

The women walk in, but Diomira is not with them. Pasqualina, Rosario's wife, is there, and so is lovely Caterina. She smiles at him, and his stomach flips. He would love to talk to her a little, in private, but no, he can't.

He dismisses that thought as if an annoying fly, then raises his glass to the other end of the table. A toast, to whomever might be over there. He cannot see the features, the light is so dim, so dark. He sees one of them, raising their glass to him, filled with wine, red wine, like a cup of blood.

Mancini, the carabinieri maresciallo.

The one next to him is still in darkness. He's wearing one of those military capes, used against the wind and rain, but it's sunny and warm outside. How strange.

He looks closer, and he thinks he recognizes him: Calabrese, that young man from out of town.

Suddenly, the sun disappears; the windows slam open, and a cold wind rushes through the room.

Maybe Calabrese was right to dress like that; maybe that's why he's smiling. No, not smiling: grinning, a grimace of hatred and evil, as evil as his bloodshot eyes glinting in the darkness.

There's a dull thud. Then another, and another. The children fall face-first onto the table, their blood staining the white tablecloth. A hatchet is in each of their heads, all lined up, their arms wide like rag dolls. Rosario's children first, then his wife, his sister-in-law, their skull split by a hatchet.

He wants to scream but his voice gets caught in his throat. He turns to his right, and Rosario is gone. His foot catches in Rosario's body, on the ground, his head detached and rolling away.

He jumps to his feet; he must save all the other children at least, his children, in the darkness where he can't see them. He calls them, one by one: "Antonio! Canio, Saverio!" No reply. "Mena! Caterina!" Nothing.

Then finally, he sees them. Lined up, hand in hand, from the eldest to the youngest. There are no scars or wounds on their bodies, but they have been touched by death. Their faces are grey, gaunt; he can see the bones on their bodies. He knows how they died, too: they starved.

The scream finally makes it out of his mouth and pours out like bile, alleviating for a moment the nausea of regret.

Oreste wakes up.

The scream pierced the night, but no one truly noticed.

Screams and cries, within those walls, were a regular occurrence on par with a rooster crowing at dawn. The patients expressed their anxieties, their delusions, their overwhelming feelings through battle cries and howls that echoed through the night even more so than the day.

And it was night-time that summoned images in Oreste's mind which daytime helped hide away; nightmares, then, were the way in which the events of the past resurfaced. This turbulent sleep pattern, the cold sweats, all of it was affecting his health by then.

His complexion would turn a shade of deep red; he would start sweating as he rambled on about this or that, shouting his monologues from the darkness of his cell, or from the common spaces when he was allowed to meet other patients.

Nurses and guards were his torturers; the medics and doctors conspired against him, to keep him in there, even though he was innocent and had to share the rest of his life with people who were actually mad, but not him, no; he was perfectly sane and lucid; he could offer something to the country; he had a plan, a design for a locomotive that used no cables (he had never even come close to an engineering notion) which would lead them to victory in the war raging beyond the walls, and the Duce would see him and help him.

In fact, he had appealed to the Duce several times and wrote letters containing his tale, asking for justice and mercy upon him and his family, victims of a premeditated trap from enemies of the government such as Mancini and De Nicola. The letters, the plans, the designs, all of them were intercepted by the director – another enemy of the Fatherland – who would discard them.

Once, on a walk in the yard, he met the director surrounded by all his acolytes and sycophants. He did not recognize his features; he didn't look anything like the man who had welcomed him to the institute years prior; he recognized the arrogance of his slow gait, his hands behind his back, his hair slicked back with pomade.

He looked like Mancini. It was Mancini. Maybe not.

He knew either way that this man was also complicit in the crimes against his family. He moved closer, approaching from behind, weaving between the pillars in the portico; he was a couple metres away, and he couldn't help himself: he went for the throat.

"You bastard! You coward! Even my niece, she was just a child!"

He pounced upon the director, foaming at the mouth and wailing accusations about facts that had never happened, the clear goal of strangling him right there and then.

Fortunately for the director, there were many people present, and all of them were used to patients lashing out. That was their job, after all. They blocked Oreste before he could even touch his intended target and before the director could even work out what had happened.

They strapped him into a straitjacket, then some extra leather straps, so tight that they would leave a mark. Oreste had become more violent recently, more of a danger to others and to himself, and they needed to secure him.

He would frequently find himself tied down to his wooden bench, silent and still, in the darkness of his cell, in the sole company of the stink of mould and rancid sweat keeping him company. Days would become weeks, weeks months; months turned into years.

Time passed, and with it so did the events shaking the world. The war had ended; history had changed through it, perhaps forever. After taking part in and causing a wide array of horrors, Italy was about to be reborn. Oreste had no idea any of this was happening, nor did many of his fellow inmates. They knew not of the war;

they knew not of its consequences. They were lesser beings, barely even human, and as such, it was not their place to know.

CHAPTER 22

Professor Filippo Saporito, director of the Judicial Asylum of Aversa, had come to Reggio Emilia for a few days. He was here from Rome, where he taught at La Sapienza university, to consult on the most notorious and sensational serial case killer of the century.

According to the Professor, one Leonarda Cianciulli – known to everyone as the soap-maker of Correggio – was to be considered not of sane mind, and therefore incapable of rational thought when she had killed three of her friends, cut them up into pieces, and melted them in lye to make soap bars out of them.

The case had become the most followed piece of news in 1946, second only to the horrors of the war. The details kept adding up every day, and public opinion was horrified and morbidly drawn to it.

Leonarda had used a hatchet (another hatchet, it's always a hatchet) to hack her victims, then had gathered their blood in a copper pot, dried it out in the oven, crumbled it into dust, and mixed it in with her cookie dough. She had served cookies with tea to her friends.

According to her, it had all been to prevent the death of her children, as they had been cursed at birth, and only the sacrifice of the innocent could help them. She claimed as such in a long report.

There was no real need for the consultation, as Leonarda Cianciulli was demonstrably insane and everyone would have agreed. The defence however had gone all out: they had ridden the wave of attention from the media and brought in the utmost expert of criminal psychology, who had already written so much about cases such as Musolino the brigand, Vincenzo Paterno – who had killed Countess Giulia Trigona of Saint Elia – and Antonio Gramsci.

Saporito had arrived in Reggio a few days before the trial and had been staying with his colleague Mario Fraulini, director of the city's Criminal Asylum.

The two were currently walking side by side along the narrow hallways between the two rows of patient cells. They were chatting, colloquially, as if taking a stroll on the beach promenade on a nice spring day. They didn't appear to care for the dead eyes and sad features watching them from each cell in the dim light of the asylum.

They had just walked past Oreste's cell, too, without stopping; his face was just one of the hundreds in this place, and they had seen many like him and many more would come. Oreste, for his part, didn't look up at the two doctors. He cared little for them, as he cared little for anything else around him.

Saporito, however, suddenly saw a spark of something, out of the corner of his eye. He turned back to look at Oreste's cell.

"I know that man," he said. "Or rather, I am pretty sure I recognize him."

Fraulini knew Solimeno well. He had caused a not insignificant amount of trouble, and he had stood out from the other patients – not to mention his prognosis was getting more concerning by the day.

"The name is Oreste Solimeno. He's a permanent guest of ours, multiple homicide, life sentence, but he's with us for paranoid dementia."

The Reggio institute director did not mention the accident from some time prior, when Oreste had almost strangled him. It would have lessened the reputation of the place and drawn unwanted scrutiny of the security and reliability of the guards.

"Solimeno. I remember a Solimeno in Salerno, or somewhere around there, that I took care of in Aversa. That one recovered, however."

Saporito's memory was still unparalleled. He seemed to be unable to forget any face, any diagnosis, any name no matter how long it had been since he had come across them. He had just done the same with Oreste; he had focused in on the subject, and the other details about the patient were slowly re-surfacing.

"The Capaccio massacre. 1921, or maybe 1922. He came to me ten years later, but I was pretty certain it was just prisoner's psychosis. I released him with a clean bill of health; I am not sure why he would still be in an asylum."

"Not much difference to us; he's in for a life sentence. If not here, he'd be in a penitentiary, locked up either way."

"No, my dear colleague. They pardoned everyone after this war, even the most ferocious criminals. If he had been in prison, he would also be free twenty-five years later."

"He's manic and paranoid. He has lost all spatio-temporal awareness, keeps bringing up conflicts between supporters of Bourbons and Sabaudi, believes himself to be a great innovator and every fifteen days demands to speak to the Duce. I've seen a decline in physical health recently too; he's aging, and I fully believe he will meet his death here."

Saporito, always insightful, noticed Fraulini's bitterness towards the patient, but his experience had taught him not to pry. He only hoped that the director's personal feelings were only involved in this one, unique case, and not a wide-spread approach in his institute.

They changed subject and kept the conversation moving, leaving Oreste behind along with the lives of the other patients, whose eyes followed them as far as they could see, as far as they could follow, and as far as a new face broke through the monotony of their days.

Saporito had been right: Fraulini had it in for Oreste specifically and had never forgotten nor forgiven the attempt on his life.

When Mario Fraulini's secretary brought the post on the morning of August 12th 1946, the director immediately spotted the letter from Saverio Solimeno, Oreste's youngest son; he was caught between immediately discarding it or granting it five minutes of his time. His curiosity prevailed.

Esteemed Director,

Only today, after long years of incarceration on returning to my homeland, my thoughts go to my father Oreste Solimeno, held in your institute.

I do not have a say, Director, about the responsibilities held by my father in the events or his claims of innocence. I write this letter so that I may inquire as to his well-being and whether there are the conditions for a pardon and subsequent release.

I believe, Director, that the pardon that so many have received may be extended to my father, considering that he has been deprived of his freedom for the past twenty-four years and that three of his children have devoted seven, nine, and three years of their youth to our country.

It goes without saying that in case of effective release, all costs of recovery and care would befall to myself and the other members of his family, including guardianship.

I dare to hope, Director, for a reply containing the details of his release and your blessing and support for anything that may be beneficial to the wellbeing of my father.

Please accept my advance thanks along with those of my entire family, and forward good wishes and words of affection to my father on our behalf as well.

Yours deferentially,
Saverio Solimeno
Torre dei Cacciatori – Paestum (Salerno)

Fraulini's lip curled with derision. He didn't even reach for the letterhead to respond, just a quickly scrawled reply on the margin of the letter from Saverio Solimeno. A response to all the uses of "Director" as if trying to hold him personally responsible.

Your father – sentenced to life for murder – is suffering from paranoid dementia and as such, should he receive a pardon, he will be transferred to a Civil Asylum. Physically he is well.

Greetings.

Asking him to send the letter back, he called back his secretary. "One other thing," he added, as the man was about to leave the office. "If any more correspondence arrives from Solimeno's family, I don't want to see it. Discard it immediately."

CHAPTER 23

Towards the end of May, when the days had started growing longer again and the evening didn't come until at least eight, patients were allowed to linger outside of their rooms, in common areas, until seven thirty.

Meals were served at noon and six no matter the season, meaning that summer evening allowed for patients depending on their needs and capabilities, to spend some time in each other's company, to socialize.

There were patients afflicted by schizophrenia, paranoia, depression; having them all in the same location at the same time could be dangerous, but was still necessary as more isolation would just undermine their already fragile minds.

As usual, Oreste was among those who made the Director regret loosening those restrictions. He was irascible, restless, and kept trying to pick fights.

Fraulini, after all this time, had somewhat softened his resentment against his patient, and had changed his approach a little. The letters from his family were no longer directly trashed; he replied to each and every one of them, and made sure that all care packages – probably gathered with not minimal amounts of effort and sacrifice – found their way to the intended destination. Fraulini had developed a form of pity for this man, out of a Christian spirit even he did not know he possessed, though he still vividly remembered the attack at his expense.

Oreste, on the other hand, kept getting worse.

His sermons had become rants, and sometimes he'd get so worked up he'd go purple in the face and almost forget to breathe.

He would then throw himself onto his bed for the rest of the day, sometimes more than one, once again ignoring everything and everyone.

The evening of May 23rd 1952, after another rambling rant about how the world would be better if those in power listened to the likes of him, something in Oreste's mind snapped. It was eight in the evening, and he had just been accompanied back to his room.

He had spent thirty of his sixty-nine years in a cell, not knowing if he was guilty – as the world had sentenced – or innocent, as his conscience would suggest once in a while.

The news arrived in Naples first, where Saverio was working for the Civil Engineering department; then it reached Ermelinda, working for a family in Posillipo, and finally Caterina, who had been a widow for the past fifteen years and whose life had worn out more than her siblings.

When she learned of her father's death, Caterina took out the nice coat from the closet, found her purse, and went to the cinema. She loved the cinema; it fascinated her; there were images; there was sound, and there was no need to know how to read.

She would've loved to have learned how to read; an entire world escaped her at her fingertips, a world that even children could decipher – but not she. She was ashamed every time she had to ask someone to help her read a simple postcard. She hated her ignorance and through it, she had hated her father – her late father – who with neither rhyme nor reason had not sent her to school, not even to learn how to write her name.

"I'll go to the cinema," she told herself. "And I'll catch the showing twice."

The *Italia* on *corso* Garibaldi was showing *Nobody's Children* with Amedeo Nazzari and Yvonne Sanson. Caterina could get there walking along *via* Enrico Cosenz, the road with the ice factory, the one commonly known as *o' rettifilo puveriello*, the lesser Rettifilo; the actual one was *corso* Umberto I, filled with stores and storefronts.

She sat through the end credits; as everyone else stood up to leave, her eyes fixed on the lines of names running along the screen.

Then, finally, she thought of her father, the man she hadn't seen in thirty years and now would never see again. In the dark cinema theatre, lit by the dim courtesy lights, where no one could see her, Caterina finally cried.

Capaccio only found out the following day, when Saverio was able to get in touch with his brother Canio and the latter told everyone else. The family, what was left of it, now lived in Torre di Paestum in the valley, not far from the beaches that had seen Operation Avalanche on September 9th 1943.

The yard outside the main building had a grape awning, and a sturdy wooden table beneath it; on top of the table was a basket filled with cherries. Fresh cherries, almost too red not to burst by looking at them, a gift from one of Canio's friends, whose contacts were improving, and with them his business.

Eliana, Canio's second born, was the youngest in the family, and as such, the most spoiled. She knew that her daddy had brought those cherries for her, but she didn't dare bring herself to take one without an adult telling her she could. Hoping for someone to appear, she admired them at a distance, but everyone seemed to have vanished.

She thought she could hear Aunt Filomena crying; she heard the words "poor father" and "Reggio Emilia" but had no idea what it all meant: the five-year old's priorities were those lovely, red, juicy looking cherries.

She tiptoed closer to the basket, looked around herself and raised a hand. Slowly but surely, Eliana ate so many cherries that afternoon, as no one ever came to stop her. They all knew they were for her alone. Eliana's memory of a grandfather she never met was all in that basket of cherries, the delicious afternoon, and the painful tummy ache she had as a result.

CHAPTER 24

August 15th – *Ferragosto* – 1959 was a Saturday.

Having a holiday and a Sunday next to each other meant that the Madonna del Granato celebrations that year drew many more people than usual.

Moving towards the basilica, climbing up the hill towards the top of Mount Calpazio, the river of people started flowing from the very early hours of the day. The basilica overlooked the entire Sele valley and had been built by Paestum during the 10th Century, after their city had been destroyed by raids two centuries prior. Marian worship had spread very quickly throughout the Cilento region.

The celebration took place on Ferragosto, the day of the Virgin Mary's Assumption, with a procession of Cente: wooden boat-shaped icons made of wreathed candles, in honour of the Madonna. The streets before the basilica were filled with stalls of sweets and nougat, preventing cars from driving through, and a *carabiniere* had been posted to redirect the sparse traffic if needed.

The man waved at the grey Fiat 1100 to stop. The driver half smiled, showed a document, and the young man stepped aside, saluting the vehicle as it drove past.

The car lurched through the crowd, low gears loudly spinning the engine and causing blue spurts of exhaust into the already stuffy summer air.

As it reached the square in front of the church, a man dressed in black stepped out of it, coat and hat very out of season. He walked around the car and helped the other, much older man out of the passenger seat.

The older man inhaled, gathering his strength, and looked around. Using the walking stick, squinting in the warm light and in the wave of memories coming back to him, he hobbled towards the low wall over the panoramic terrace.

Antonio Bertolucci, former *appuntato* of the Royal *Carabinieri,* had the bad legs and uncertain gait of the eighty-year old, but his mind was still fresh and young; *those events* specifically were still at the forefront, too.

His son Giuseppe, who had driven him up here, was Police commissioner in Foggia. Twenty years later had been able to fulfill his father's wishes to go back to Capaccio.

The procession streamed before their eyes, with the Cente raised high, their ribbons fluttering in the air. As the Madonna passed by them, father and son removed their hats and signed themselves.

"As the crowd thins, please take me down again," the old man said.

"Are you sure, dad?" his son replied, concerned that his heart might not hold. "It's been so long; isn't it easier for those folks to put all of it behind?"

"Please, let's go. I've waited too long already; I don't want to die with the regret of never having said anything."

Giuseppe had found out where the people his father wanted to see were living these days. They needed to head into Torre de' Cacciatori, which had changed its name to Torre di Paestum. Twenty minutes by car, slowly to ensure the old man didn't tire.

He was almost certain they would find some of the men home, too, given the holidays. He was looking for the children of Oreste Solimeno.

The tower that gave its name to the town had been built in the sixteenth century to aid against raiders and invasions, and later – ironically – used by the Germans against the Allies during the 1943 operation. In any other part of the world, the structure would have been a national monument; here it was nothing more than a ruin. Right across from it was a small *bar*, a café, anonymous, with a couple of metal tables and chairs right outside it.

Its walls were covered in brand names like *Peroni*, *Campari*, even *Drink Coca-Cola*: the feeling was definitely one of a summer *bar*, and though the economic boom had yet to hit Italy fully, there was a light-heartedness that very few had felt before in the air.

There were even people traipsing down to the beach, a single cotton towel over their shoulder, and no shoes despite the sharp stones and rocks.

The tables were full, occupied by three pairs of card players, laughing and playing for the 'half beer' prize that had become tradition.

Giuseppe Bertolucci parked the 1100 on the right side of the road and headed straight for one of the tables. His father watched him with pride and could see himself thirty or forty years earlier, when he still had the youth and the strength, but also the experience, to do his daily duties as a *carabiniere*.

Had he always done his duty? He thought so, or at least, he had tried to do so. The only regret that gnawed at him, and had gnawed at him for a long time was that he was never able to secure the actual culprits for that terrible murder, despite his hunch and gut telling him he knew he had the wrong person.

He saw one of the men standing around the players raise his hand, pointing at one of the houses further up the street, and saw his son thank him and head back to the car.

"We're here," Giuseppe said, "Just a little ahead."

"Did you ask if any of the sons are home?"

"Canio should be, yes. He was at the *bar* not long ago and said he was heading home. That's what they told me at least. It is a holiday after all; the whole family might be there."

They found him in the front yard of the large house. He welcomed them with the smile typical of those times, where everything felt as though it was finally being reborn. That, and Canio was already a happy, jovial man: if you ever paid a visit to ask for a favour, he would offer you food first, then do the favour, then realize he hadn't even asked for your name.

Giuseppe Bertolucci stepped out of the car.

"Mister Solimeno, good morning," he said, as he offered his hand. "My name is Giuseppe Bertolucci, police commissioner in Foggia."

Canio looked concerned for a moment. He thought of his son Oreste, in his twenties and a known hothead – had he gotten into trouble?

"Has Oreste done something?" he blurted, though he had no idea what his son might be doing in Foggia.

"No, please, don't worry. This is about your father Oreste, not your son."

"My father died seven years ago, commissioner, and not in his own bed. It's a long story."

"Yes, we're aware. I just have some additional details that I don't believe you are privy to."

Canio's smile reappeared, overwhelming any other feeling the words might have stirred.

"Please, let's sit under the arbour; it's cooler."

"My father is the one who would like to speak with you; he's waiting in the car."

"Well, let him out! It's way too hot."

He reached the car himself and opened the passenger side door. "My name is Canio Solimeno," he greeted the old man. "Please, come with me to the shade."

"Canio. Baby Canio. I remember you at the age of ten. You don't remember me, do you? It's been so long. So much has changed – people, times, the world."

"Mister Bertolucci, please, come sit. You too, commissioner. I'll be right back with something to drink."

He left them alone, listening in silence to the waves murmuring not far from the house. He returned with three glasses and a ceramic pitcher of lemonade.

"Canio is not a common name around here," Giuseppe said, after a few sips. "It reminds me of a Leoncavallo opera, *Pagliacci*."

"It's uncommon around most places," Canio replied. "That's just what my father was like. He enjoyed peculiar names once the traditions were fulfilled. There are eight of us, so he had free rein after the fourth. I believe mine might actually be from that opera. My mother told me he enjoyed Leoncavallo."

"Your father had his quirks; this is true. My dad knew him best, though, so perhaps we should let him speak instead."

Antonio Bertolucci rummaged in his coat pocket and took out a yellowed piece of folded paper. "This is a letter for your uncle, I believe Enrico," he said, as he handed it over to Canio. "Giuseppe Di Miele wrote it in June 1931."

"Di Miele. One of the De Nicola murderers." Canio stated, didn't ask.

"One of the actual killers, yes. Please, read it."

Dearest Cousin...

His face hardened, his features darkening as he kept reading, his breathing increasing.

"This clears his name. This would have cleared his name once and for all; why is it only now coming to light? Thirty years! Dear God, he was locked up for thirty years, and he was innocent!"

"Maybe," the commissioner corrected him. "He might have been innocent. There is no proof as to whether the letter is genuine, and there is no proof as to whether its contents are truthful. In any case, the trial was a shambles, the motive practically non-existent, and this letter just opens up a whole new series of doubts."

Bertolucci father raised his hand, as if to tell his son to let him speak instead.

"Canio, I am here because you and your family have a right to know and so that I may die without the regret of having kept quiet. That letter arrived in Capaccio in 1932, directly at the *Carabinieri* barracks as a piece of evidence to add to the file, but no other instruction. They had probably sequestered it from Di Miele who, I believe, had never been able to send it. At the time, the murders had faded from memory a little; it had been ten years, and I was the only one left. Mancini had long been transferred and the new commander cared very little about a fact from before his time. He ordered me to file it away, as I knew where we kept everything. When I picked up the file, everything came back to me. All the incongruences, the lies, the false evidence. Everything revealed itself to me just as it had back then. I always believed Oreste to be innocent, but I was never able to demonstrate it."

"So? What did you do?" Canio asked.

"I folded the letter just like it was when I handed it to you. I slid it into my pocket and closed the file again and hid it as far back in the archive as I could. I thought I would be able to do something about it sooner or later, but the truth is that much like everyone else involved, I did nothing."

"What could you have done, dad?" Giuseppe interjected. "Reopen the case? Start the trial again after Oreste had already been declared insane?"

"The times weren't easy," the old man continued. "The entire justice system was a branch of the Fascist regime; everything had to take place according to the new rules, and a Fascist tribunal would never dare undo what another Fascist tribunal had done. I kept the letter, dreaming of better days, which never came. The war, deployment, evacuations, everything we've all had to go through until not long ago."

"But now, what good can this letter do?" Canio said. "Unless any of my siblings want to re-open the trial posthumously. And even so, between lawyers, bureaucracy, we wouldn't even know where to start or how to pay for it. We can't do anything. We won't do anything; we always knew he was innocent."

"I believe you're doing the right thing," Giuseppe agreed. "I can see that the Solimeno family is well liked in town again; no one I asked for directions made any comments, openly or subtly, no allusions."

"Seven years after his death, trying to bring everything back up. No, I don't think that's best."

Canio stood up. The conversation had been civil, and calm, but he was still shaken, and he wanted nothing more than to bid farewell to those two people appearing from the past.

The old man stood up also, using his cane, and his son offered him an arm to reach the car once more.

"One last thing, actually; your mother, Diomira?" he asked, fully expecting bad news.

Canio did not reply but gestured to both of them to follow him inside.

Weaving through the braids over the door meant to keep out flies and other bugs, they stepped into a cool kitchen, half in shade.

Diomira was asleep on an armchair, a cushion behind her back. She was staring ahead of her, her gaze and mind lost who knows where.

"Ma," Canio called her. "There are two friends here to see you."

The woman barely turned her head.

"She's been like this for the past year," Canio explained. "The doctors say it was a stroke. She barely recognizes any of us."

Antonio Bertolucci looked at the woman, felt a great sadness wash over him, and fought the tears coming to his eyes. He was unable to speak.

They turned back to leave, when they heard a soft murmur.

Diomira slowly raised an arm, as if to wave in their direction. Then, her voice nothing more than a whisper and a thread of drool coming out the corner of her mouth, she spoke the same words she had said to Bertolucci thirty-seven years earlier.

"*Appuntato,* thank you."

Matteo Dello Schiavo was born in Naples in 1968, but his family is from Capaccio (in the province of Salerno, in the Campania region of south-western Italy), where he lives. He pursued classical studies, has a degree in Economics, and is an inspector in the Guardia di Finanza (the Italian finance police). Married to Maria, he has two children of whom he is very proud.

Alex Valente (he/him) is a white European currently living on xʷməθkʷəy̓əm, Sḵwx̱wú7mesh, and səlilwətaɬ land. He is a literary translator from Italian into English, though he also dabbles with French and RPGs, and is co-editor of *The Norwich Radical*. His work has been published in *NYT Magazine*, *The Massachusetts Review*, *The Short Story Project*, and *PEN Transmissions*.